An Amish H

By Diana Morgan

This is a work of fiction. Names, characters, and incidents are products of the writer's imagination and are not to be construed as real. Any resemblance to actual events or persons, living or dead, is entirely coincidental.

An Amish Heart

Copyright@2014 by Diana Morgan

In loving memory of my brother, Michael Dunk.

Glossary

bopplies: *baby*

daed: *dad*

danke: *thank you*

Englisch: *Someone who is not Amish.*

grossdaadi haus: *grandparents' home on the property.*

Guder Mariye: *Good Morning*

gut: *good*

haus: *house*

jah: *yes*

kaffi: *coffee*

kapp: *woman's head covering*

mamm: *mom*

meddaagesse: *noon meal*

menner: *men*

nee: *no*

schul: *school*

sohn: *son*

Prologue

LaGrange County, Indiana

Ella Graber carefully tiptoed into her father's office and froze. From the living room she could hear the soft murmur of her parent's voices as they discussed the day's events and from the kitchen, the quiet squabbling of her sisters as they went about their evening chores.

She breathed a sigh of relief. The last thing she needed was to have her plans foiled before they had even begun.

"Ella?" Corrine, her four-year-old sister, peeked around the corner of the door. "What are you doing?"

Ella placed a finger to her lips as a signal for her sister to be quiet. "Nothing, Corrine. Now go into the kitchen and tell Holly I said you can have one of the oatmeal cookies you helped me bake this morning."

Corrine grinned, her blue eyes twinkling. "Can I have two?" she whispered.

Ella smiled softly at her little sister. "*Jah*," she said and made a shooing motion. "You can have two." She watched as her little sister scampered down the hall then turned back to the task at hand.

Her father's sturdy oak desk, built by her grandfather many years ago, stood against the far wall. It had been a fixture in the room for as long as she could remember and she had spent many rainy afternoons playing with her dolls on its polished surface.

With shaking hands she grasped the desk's top drawer and eased it open. The keys to her Ford

Taurus gleamed in the faint moonlight that streamed through the office window. She quickly scooped them up, deposited them inside the pocket of her apron and smiled.

Her father hadn't approved of her purchase of the car even though many Amish youth drove vehicles during their *rumspringa,* a time beginning at the age of sixteen when the young people were given permission to experience the outside world before becoming baptized members of the church.

He had forced her to park the car behind the barn until he could list it for sale in the local paper. And that is where it currently sat, hidden from view.

"The car shall remain parked." Her normally easy-going *daed* had snapped when she had protested. His brown eyes had flashed with disapproval. "You have no business racing this thing up and down the county roads. You are eighteen, Ella. You need to focus on joining the church and settling down."

"*Jah, Daed,*" she had murmured, but in her heart she knew she would take the old Ford out for one last drive.

"Ella? Did you remember to take your medicine?" *Mamm* called from the living room.

"I'm going to take it now, *Mamm*." Ella tip toed down the hall and eased open the screen door leading to the back porch. The hinges groaned in protest as she squeezed through and closed it softly behind her.

For a brief moment she felt a pang of guilt for lying to her mother. She hadn't taken the medicine to treat her bipolar disorder for over a week, slipping the pills into the trash when her family wasn't looking.

She hated the way the medicine made her feel, as if all joy had been sucked out of life. She much preferred to ride the wave of a manic high with its unexpected twists and turns.

Ella smiled as she twirled in a circle and happily breathed in the evening air washed clean by a late afternoon thunderstorm. To the west, lightening flashed and she could hear the distant rumble of thunder signaling the arrival of an impending storm.

Holding her breath, she eased along the side of the house and ducked as she passed the kitchen window. The window was open to the cool night air and she could hear her sisters, Holly and Faith argue over whose turn it was to wash the dishes.

Ella giggled and had to smother a laugh as their discussion became heated. It was really her turn to wash the dishes, but she wasn't about to miss out on an evening of fun. Besides, she had completed her sisters' chores plenty of times when they had stayed overnight with friends.

With a quick glance back at the house, she raced across the yard until she reached the barn's side door. Easing it open, she stepped into the cool interior and listened. Her older *bruder*, Isaac, often came to the barn in the evenings to finish up chores. She couldn't risk him putting an end to her carefully made plans.

The barn was quiet. Ella could hear her horse, Midnight, stirring in his stall, but there was no sign of her nosey, older brother. She breathed a sigh of relief and gingerly made her way through the barn's thick shadows.

Midnight nickered a greeting and Ella walked over to say hello to the dappled gray. If animals could be considered friends, he was one of the best. She leaned over to drop a kiss on his soft nose and paused to wrap her arms around his sturdy neck. Sometimes Ella felt as if her pet was the only living creature in the entire world who understood her.

Her mother and father certainly didn't understand her. They considered her to be too outspoken and too lax with the Amish ways. She wasn't quiet and obedient like her sister, Holly, nor steadfast in her faith like her *bruder,* Isaac.

Giving Midnight one last pat, Ella stepped into a far corner and reached for the clothes she had carefully hidden that afternoon. Pulling out the bundle, she quickly extracted a pair of low rise jeans and her favorite moss green sweater.

Noah always liked it when she wore green. He said it brought out the green in her eyes.

Just the thought of the six foot two Noah Wyse with his wavy dark hair and vivid blue eyes brought a smile to Ella's face. Noah had an identical twin brother, Caleb, but while Caleb was nice looking, she secretly believed Noah to be the more handsome of the two.

She had loved him since second grade when he had prevented Ezra King from pelting her with snowballs filled with bits of dirt and leaves. Noah had been in sixth grade and was spending the recess hanging out with his large group of friends, but he had taken the time to come to her rescue. Her young heart had melted and she had spent the next several years tagging after him until two years ago when he had begun to notice that she wasn't a little girl any longer.

Noah had been nervous the first time he had asked if he could take her home in his buggy after a singing. He had hemmed and hawed until he finally was able to get the words out of his mouth.

Ella smiled at the memory as she quickly changed her clothes, stashing her *kapp*, dress and apron in a corner before slipping out the barn's back door. She stopped to listen for any sounds from the house, and sighed in relief when she heard none. If her sisters had noticed she was missing, they hadn't raised an alarm.

She walked with careful steps and crossed the few feet to where her car was parked. The fire engine red sedan shone in the moonlight and she ran her hand over the smooth finish, saddened that this would be her last chance to drive the vehicle. Their neighbor had offered to pay fifteen hundred for the car and her father had readily accepted.

Ella couldn't help, but smile as she unlocked the door and slid behind the wheel. How she loved this car. She had worked long hours at the local market to earn enough money to purchase a vehicle and was a little put out that her father was making her sell it.

She knew she would have to get rid of the car before she became a baptized member of the church, but taking one last drive couldn't hurt. She brushed aside the feeling of guilt she felt for disobeying her father and inserted the key into the ignition.

Ella shivered in anticipation as she put the car in gear and allowed it to roll forward across the pasture toward the gravel road running in front of the house. Only when the car was a safe distance down the road, did she release the breath she had been holding and flip on the headlights.

Noah would be surprised to see her. He didn't approve of her driving a car, but she knew he wouldn't turn down her request to go for one last joy ride.

With barely contained glee, Ella pressed her foot down on the accelerator and laughed as the old car surged forward into the darkness.

This was going to be a night to remember.

She rolled down the window, letting the cool spring air whip her auburn hair into a wild tangle about her head. She would have an awful time later that evening combing the snarls out of her hair and setting it to right, but for now it was worth it.

She shivered in excitement as she reached down and turned on the radio, humming along to a popular country song before checking her makeup in the rear view mirror. She was grateful her mother and father couldn't see her. Her parents had been good about looking the other way when she wore just a hint of lip gloss, but neither would approve of the heavy eye shadow and bright red lipstick that adorned her youthful face.

Ella knew the community thought she was wild and out of control. She had often heard whispers condemning her reckless behavior, but she didn't care. All that mattered was the opinion of one man and Noah Wyse thought she could do no wrong.

She took a curve too fast, the car's tires sliding on the loose gravel before slowing down for a stop sign. She turned right onto the narrow paved road leading to the Wyse farm and quickly accelerated, laughing as the car roared through the quiet countryside. She had never liked the slowness of riding in a buggy, much preferring the *Englisch* mode of transportation.

Her cell phone rang and Ella glanced down to read the incoming text. If her father had known she had purchased a phone, he would have taken it along with the car keys, but that was information she intended to keep to herself. One never knew when a phone might come in handy, especially in this day and age.

The text was from her friend, Beverly, who was also on her *rumspringa.* Beverley's parents were far more lenient, often allowing their daughter to date and attend movies with her *Englisch* friends.

Ella smiled at the text and tossed the phone on to the passenger seat. She looked back at the road as the car crested a slight rise and slammed on the brakes, but it was too late. The car's tires slid on the wet pavement, doing little to slow the vehicle down before it plowed into the back of the buggy turning into the Wyse's drive.

She closed her eyes against the horrifying sight as she heard a sickening crunch and a horse's scream. In a moment it was over. Her car ended up in a ditch, while what was left of the buggy sat in a mangled heap in the middle of the road.

A blanket of silence settled over the scene as Ella unfastened her seatbelt and prepared to witness the destruction she had caused.

The hinges of the car door groaned in protest as she slowly opened it and stepped out into the coolness of the night. A slight breeze ruffled her hair as she took a step forward.

There was a loud shout from the direction of the house.

Ella turned as a dark figure raced past.

Her legs shook as she followed. She could see the body of Noah's father, Silas Wyse, hanging from the ruins of the buggy. By the twisted angle of his neck and unseeing eyes, she could tell he was dead.

Ella whispered a prayer.

Glass from the car's broken headlights crunched underneath her feet as she walked by the buggy, passing the still twitching body of the Wyse's faithful horse. Just ahead, she could see a figure crouched beside a body lying in the road.

It had begun to rain again. Large droplets of water pelted down around her as she stared in disbelief at the face of the injured man. It was not until the crouching figure rose, then turned, that she realized it was Caleb lying in the middle of the road and not Noah.

Ella felt a moment of relief and then shame for feeling grateful that Noah had been spared when two members of his family had not. How could she ever forgive herself for what she had done?"

Noah met her gaze, his blue eyes glazed with pain. His face twisted in grief as he let out a strangled sob.

"It was an accident," she whispered, but her words became lost in the wind.

Tears streamed down Noah's face as he turned away from her.

Ella gazed in horror at Caleb. His eyes were closed and a large puddle of blood had begun to form beneath his head, mingling with the falling rain.

"Forgive me, God," she whispered as she took a staggering step back. She felt herself begin to fall before her world faded to black.

Chapter One

Six years later.

Indianapolis, Indiana

Sometimes Ella dreamed about him. The way his dark hair tumbled over his forehead and the azure blue of his eyes. His smile haunted her and she often heard the deep timbre of his voice as it floated through her dreams, whispering of times long past. She would awaken with tears in her eyes, his name on her lips as she stared into the darkness and thought about what could have been.

The shrill ringing of her cell phone pierced the night and left her stumbling to the kitchen to retrieve it from where she had left it the evening before.

"Ella?" Her mother's voice echoed down the phone line and across the miles separating LaGrange County from Indianapolis. "There's been a terrible accident." She paused for a moment, as if to collect her thoughts. "Isaac is dead."

Ella sank down onto the nearest chair as she pictured her older brother the way he had looked during his last visit. He had sat in this very spot, his brown eyes filled with concern as he attempted to persuade her to return home.

She hadn't listened.

"Ella?"

"I'm here," she said, her voice choked with emotion. She gave a cursory swipe at the hot tears which had begun to trail down her cheeks. "What happened?"

Her mother hesitated. "He died in a buggy accident coming home from work yesterday. His buggy was broadsided by a van when it slid on ice and went through an intersection."

Ella gasped. Immediately her mind transported her back six years to another accident that had ended in death. One that had shattered far too many lives and crushed youthful dreams.

"How is Susan?" she whispered. Sweet-tempered Susan, Isaac's wife and her best friend, although time and distance had taken a toll on their friendship.

Six years ago Susan had been dating Caleb. They had often joked that after she married Caleb and Ella married Noah, they would live side by side and their children would grow up together.

"She's in shock," her mother's voice was laced with tears. "We all are, but I worry about how this will affect the *bopplies*. Susan's doctor put her on bed rest a couple of months ago, but I pray this added stress doesn't cause harm."

"Babies?"

"*Jah.* Twins. Didn't Isaac and Susan tell you?"

"*Nee.*" Isaac had made no mention of it during his visit. Ella tried to put aside the hurt she felt at being kept in the dark. After all, she had been the one who had placed distance between herself and her family.

"When is she due?"

"In February, but since she is expecting twins, it could be sooner." Her mother sighed. "Susan keeps saying she wants to move to Kentucky and live with her brother and his family. I'm afraid that after the funeral, she will leave. Maybe if you come home she will decide to stay. The two of you use to be close."

They had been.

Ella thought back to her childhood and all the secrets she and Susan had shared. They had spent many sleepovers giggling about boys, but that was a lifetime ago and she seriously doubted if her presence would be enough to change the mind of her friend.

"Tell Susan, I'm sorry." She stared out her apartment window at the dark January night, thinking about how different her family would be without her brother's calming presence.

"I will, but you can tell her yourself when you come home for your *bruder's* funeral."

Ella hesitated. "*Mamm*...I don't think..."

"You *are* coming home for your brother's funeral, Ella Graber, even if I have to send your dad and Uncle Melvin to Indianapolis to fetch you," her mother said in a no nonsense tone. "You have hidden from your family and your past for far too long."

Ella knew her mother spoke the truth. She had stayed away from her family and community, only going back a couple of times in the past six years. After the accident she had put as much distance as she could between herself and LaGrange County. Although most members in the community had offered forgiveness, she couldn't help but hear the whispers and feel the pointed stares whenever she entered a room.

At the funerals for Silas and Caleb Wyse, Noah had declined to speak to her. Ella had stood by the graves and cried as her former beau had turned his back and walked away.

So, she had left.

She had moved to Merrillville, completed her GED and been accepted into Purdue University's elementary education program. It had been a struggle, but after four years and many tears, she had graduated with a bachelor degree.

Ella had been proud and had happily written home, informing her parents of her accomplishment. But her heart had broken when her parents refused to attend her graduation. The Amish frowned upon education and deemed it unnecessary passed the eighth grade. After that, the Amish youth were schooled at home. The girls learned how to run a household, while the boys learned how to farm or one of the many trades that were allowed by the community.

A couple of months later, Holly had written to inform her that Noah had married Rebecca Lapp. Ella's tears had dripped on to the page and blurred the letter's words, rendering them unreadable. Her childish dreams of a happy ending had been crushed and she immersed herself in her life with a renewed fervor.

A year later Holly had written again to tell her that Noah and Rebecca had welcomed their first child. A baby boy they named Luke. Even though her heart was broken, Ella only wished the best for her former beau.

A third letter had arrived and Ella's heart sank when she learned that Rebecca had passed away a few months after the birth of their son from a sudden cardiac arrest. She ached for Noah and the pain he was having to endure, but she knew he was surrounded by the unwavering support of family and community.

Ella had lain awake in the dark of the night and wondered if she should return home and try to pick up the pieces of her former life, but her new life beckoned. How could she throw away the years she had invested in her education? She knew that she couldn't. Tears had filled her eyes as she prayed for Noah and the *boppli,* Luke. She asked the Lord to comfort them and help them heal from the devastating loss.

Ella had moved to Indianapolis and applied for positions in the Indianapolis School System. She had been elated when her hard work paid off and she was offered a job teaching second grade at one of the elementary schools.

She had loved interacting with her students and helping young minds learn. She hadn't even minded the long hours and low pay, but had looked forward to each new day as a chance to positively influence the next generation.

All of that had come to an abrupt end right before the winter break when she missed too many days of work due to her problems with anxiety and depression. While the school administration had been sympathetic, they had gone ahead with their decision to relieve her of her position.

Ella looked around her cramped apartment. She was two months behind on rent and in danger of being evicted.

"Ella? I'm waiting for your answer." The tone of her mother's voice left no room for argument.

"I'll be there, *Mamm*," Ella said, before hanging up the phone. "I'll be there," she whispered again to the empty apartment awash in dawn's early shadows. Even if going home meant she would run into the one person she had spent the past six years avoiding.

Noah Wyse.

Chapter Two

LaGrange County, Indiana

Ella turned her Honda Civic onto the narrow county road her family had nicknamed home lane. Behind the vehicle was a trailer packed with all her belongings. The trailer bounced and dipped as she carefully navigated around potholes created by Indiana's harsh winter.

Only a few hours had passed since she pulled her car onto I-65 and headed north, but it seemed like an eternity. Rural LaGrange County was a far cry from the hustle and bustle of downtown Indianapolis. If she were honest, she much preferred the calm and quiet to the constant noise of the big city.

On either side of the road the fields lay barren, blanketed under a thick covering of snow. Ella pictured how they would look in springtime with the new seedlings pushing up out of the rich brown earth. Spring was her favorite time of year when all of the countryside appeared touched by God's gracious hand. Living in a large city the past few years, she had missed seeing the farmland awaken to new life, but this spring would be different. This time, she would once again be at her parents' farm. Immersed in the life she had vowed to leave behind for good.

She passed the large oak tree where she and Isaac had hung a rope swing one summer. Tears blurred her vision as she remembered how her brother had laughed, his eyes dancing as he swung toward the blue sky.

Ella and her brother had been close. It was hard to believe she had allowed the once strong bond to whither, but now it was too late. Never again would she hear the warmth in his voice or be able to lean on his quiet strength. She swallowed the lump in her throat. She may have been absent from her *bruder's* life over the past few years, but at least she had the memories of the laughter and fun they had shared as children.

Ella could picture his teasing grin as they played in mounds of fallen leaves or waded in the neighbor's pond. She remembered how she had shrieked when Isaac had placed a tadpole on her head and his ensuing laughter. She would miss those times, but would treasure them always.

A few minutes later, Ella turned the car down the long driveway leading to her childhood home. Built by her great-grandfather, the two-story farmhouse stood on a small hill against the backdrop of a dreary winter sky.

She had missed this place over the years. The house had sheltered several generations of Grabers and had always been filled with warmth, laughter and love. Ella smiled as she remembered preparing holiday meals with her mother and grandmother and listening to scripture at her father's knee. These would always be precious memories, ones she would cherish for the rest of her life.

The large barn sat off to the right, its gravel area in front lined with rows of buggies and a few cars. It was hard to believe her horse, Midnight, wouldn't be in his stall, but Holly had written a couple of years ago to say that Midnight had passed away during the winter from pneumonia. Ella had felt a pang of regret that she hadn't been here to comfort her beloved pet, but found solace when Holly mentioned he hadn't suffered.

Her anxiety level began to rise as she parked the car next to an SUV. She was grateful her car wasn't the only vehicle, for it would have been a glaring reminder that she was no longer a member of the close knit community. She was an outsider. She would be treated politely, but wouldn't be allowed into their inner circle.

According to Holly, the members of the community still talked about the accident and she often heard Ella's name spoken in hushed whispers. A few of them even claimed she was crazy just like their Aunt Hannah.

Their father's sister had wandered away from home one bitterly cold night wearing only a thin layer of clothing. Her lifeless body had been found the next morning in the neighbor's pond. The official story was that she had accidently drowned, but the rumor mill spread ugly gossip about how she had taken her own life.

Ella remembered her Aunt as being vivacious and full of life. She had loved to laugh and would often spend Sunday afternoons regaling her nephew and nieces with tales from her childhood.

There had been a dark side to their Aunt Hannah as well. She had suffered for years from bipolar disorder and it was because of this that Abram Graber had been willing to have Ella tested when she began to show signs of anxiety and depression in her early teens. He had lost a sister to the horrible illness, he couldn't risk losing a daughter.

Ella wished she had given her father more credit for seeking help for her all those years ago. He had given her nothing but love and support and in return she had given him grief.

She smoothed back her auburn hair, checking in the rear view mirror to see if any tendrils had escaped the severe bun she had twisted the mass of curls in to that morning. With nervous hands she brushed imaginary bits of lint off her black sweater and skirt.

Taking a deep breath, Ella existed the vehicle and landed directly in the path of an oncoming buggy. The driver gave a shout of warning, then veered around her to pull into line next to the other buggies. He jumped down and turned her way.

Ella ducked her head and blushed as she recognized the dark haired man with piercing blue eyes. Her pulse began to race.

"Ella?" A frown marred Noah Wyse's handsome features. He started toward her across the snow and ice, but was intercepted by a couple of teenage boys offering to stable his horse.

Ella took advantage of the moment and hurried toward the house, but not before seeing Noah reach and help a blond haired woman alight from the buggy. He nodded as he bent his head to listen to what his companion had to say.

A pang of jealousy tore at her heart and she immediately felt foolish. Of course Noah had moved on with his life. He was now a widower with a son and would be searching for a woman to fulfill the role of wife and mother.

For a brief moment Ella wished that woman could be her, but then pushed the dream aside. She doubted Noah would welcome her with open arms even if he claimed to have forgiven her.

She thought back to a letter her mother had written a few months ago, telling her that Noah had begun courting Megan Zehr. Her husband had been killed in a barn raising accident the year before, leaving behind Megan as well as their two small children.

Megan had been *Englisch* before she met her husband, Josephus at a restaurant where they both worked. Josephus had left the Amish community when he was a teenager and when he decided to return, Megan had moved with him.

Megan had blond hair and blue eyes and Ella could understand how Noah might be attracted to the beautiful widow, but that didn't make seeing them together any easier. She pushed aside her feelings of jealousy and vowed to be polite to the couple.

Stunned, Noah stood beside his buggy. He didn't know why it surprised him to see Ella. Of course she would want to attend her *bruder's* funeral, but seeing her brought back feelings he didn't wish to address at the moment.

Megan placed a hand on his arm. "You didn't expect to see her, did you?"

Noah ran a hand over his jaw. "*Nee*, but I guess it's to be expected that Ella would want to return to support Susan and her family during this difficult time." He turned to help his mother as well as his young son down from the buggy. He smiled at Luke and then offered his mother an arm to lean on.

Martha Wyse shook her head. "I know this isn't the time nor the place to speak of this, but you need to give Ella Graber a wide berth while she is here. Trouble follows that girl wherever she goes and we've had more than enough over the past few years."

Noah clutched Luke's hand as he walked with his mother and Megan to the house. He knew his mother was right. If he had a brain cell left in his head he would steer clear of the pretty redhead, but he knew it wouldn't be easy. His heart was telling him one thing while his head was telling him another and at the moment he wasn't certain which one would be victorious.

Ella glanced back at Noah and then hurried up the porch steps. She paused outside the porch door and said a quick prayer asking for guidance and strength. From inside she could hear the quiet murmur of voices and recognized the deep baritone of her father.

She wiped away the tears beginning to form in the corners of her eyes. It had been a long time since she had witnessed her father's calm leadership. He had always been a safe port in a storm and many times over the past few years she had found herself wishing she could ask him for advice or just sit still and absorb his quiet strength. She knew that strength would be most evident now, as he stood by her mother as they worked through their grief over the loss of their first born.

Ella took a deep breath as she opened the outside door and steeled herself as she stepped into the warm kitchen bustling with activity.

How she had missed this place. So many memories had been formed in this very room.

Memories of countless meals shared with family and friends. And underneath it all like an invisible thread that bound them all together was an endless supply of love.

Her mother stood in the midst of a group of women. Though she was still young, only in her forties, the past six years had taken a toll. Gray hair was now interwoven with the auburn hair not covered by her *kapp* and fine lines were etched around eyes that were identical to Ella's own.

Ella wondered how much of her mother's gray hair had been the result of her worrying over her oldest daughter. She figured she already knew the answer to the question, but it didn't stop her from wishing things could have been different.

She had been selfish in leaving and even more selfish when she allowed so much time to pass before contacting her family. The years had somehow rolled by, one into the other until she found herself straying further and further from her home and the values she once held so dear.

Her mother's eyes widened. With a choked sob, she rushed across the room to give her a hug. "It's so *gut* to see you."

"Why is she here?" an anonymous voice whispered.

"Hush, now," someone else murmured. "She is here because of her *bruder*."

Ella glanced wildly from one face to another. Most wore expressions of pity, but a few stared at her with open contempt. Her surroundings faded as she backed slowly toward the door. It had been a mistake coming here. She had been a fool to think the community would accept her back with open arms.

She could see Gideon Wyse, Noah's younger brother, standing in the doorway leading to the parlor. He glared at her with hate filled eyes before turning his back.

Ella felt as if she had been stabbed. She brushed aside her mother's protests and blindly reached for the door handle, jumping in surprise as her hand came into contact with a crisp shirt and the muscled warmth underneath. She turned, her eyes locking with Noah's concerned gaze.

"Welcome home, Ella." He gave a curt nod. "I was sorry to hear about Isaac. He was a *gut* friend and will be missed."

Ella closed her eyes as his deep voice washed over her, reminding her of calmer days filled with dreams of the future. A future she had shattered in an instant.

"*Jah.* Welcome, Ella." Megan's soft voice came from behind Noah.

She stepped forward and gave Ella a sad smile. "I can't believe Isaac is gone. He would often stop by to see if the children and I needed anything from town."

Ella wasn't surprised to learn this information. Her brother had been a kind and generous man who had often gone out of his way to help those in need.

Noah cleared his throat. "Please, let me know if there is anything I can do for your family."

Ella was at a loss for words, standing so close to the man who had once been the center of her world. A man she had wounded and left behind. "*Danke,*" she finally managed to whisper.

He nodded.

She met Noah's gaze once again. "I was sorry to hear about your wife's passing."

Pain flickered in his eyes and then was gone. "*Danke* for your kind words." He pulled a little boy forward. "This is my son, Luke."

"Hello," Ella whispered, stunned by how much Luke resembled his father.

Luke stared up at her with big blue eyes before shyly retreating behind Noah's pant leg.

Noah looked at her apologetically. "Sorry. He hasn't had much experience with strangers."

His words hit her like a blow. She was a stranger now not only to this little boy, but to the entire community. She watched as Noah steered Luke around her and moved further into the room.

Ella had the distinct feeling she had been dismissed. Not that she could blame him. Why on earth had one of the first things out of her mouth been about his wife's untimely death?

She turned to find herself face to face with Martha Wyse. Martha frowned, but gave a nod of acknowledgement before crossing the kitchen to hug Ella's mother.

"Ah, there you are." Her father walked up from behind and wrapped her in a warm hug. "We were worried the snow that fell last night would cause you problems driving."

Ella shook her head and allowed herself to sink into the safety of her father's embrace. Out of the corner of her eye, she could see Noah and Megan as they offered her mother their condolences.

"I'm so sorry about Isaac, *Daed*," Ella whispered as tears streaked silently down her cheeks.

Her father cleared his throat and patted her on the back before stepping away. "*Jah, vell,* it was *Got's* will. We must not question it." His look of sadness belied his words.

Grandmother Graber placed her cheek next to Ella's. "We are so happy to have you home."

Grandfather Graber, leaning heavily on his cane, walked up to both of them and patted Ella on the back. "Welcome home, Ella." His voice was gruff, but Ella detected a hint of moisture in his eyes.

"Ella! You're home."

Ella turned and was quickly surrounded by her sisters; Holly, Faith and Corrine.

Eighteen year old Faith stepped forward and gave her a quick hug. "It's *gut* to have you home, Ella. I just wish Isaac was here to see you. He always hoped you would return to us someday."

Ella's eyes once again filled with tears as she thought about their easy going brother. It was hard to believe she would never hear his laugh again or be the recipient of one of his infectious smiles.

"Ach, Faith," twenty-two year old Holly admonished. "You didn't need to make Ella cry. We are all sad, to be sure, but now she is going to wish she hadn't returned home."

Ella's sisters' voices faded as she took a step away. She secretly wished for some time alone to collect her scattered thoughts and calm her emotions, but knew that would be impossible.

She glanced around the room. She could still hear the whispers from former neighbors and friends, and could very well imagine what they were saying.

Iris Burkholder, the bishop's wife, patted her on the shoulder. "Now don't you listen to malicious words," the elderly woman whispered. "People will talk and say cruel things, but you just keep your head up and ignore them. Your parents need you here now."

"*Danke,* Iris," she murmured. Her heart warmed at the wise woman's kind words.

Ten-year-old Corrine tugged on her sleeve. "Do you want to go upstairs and see Susan? She is lying down and wanted me to let her know the moment you arrived."

Ella glanced down at her little sister. Solemn blue eyes gazed up at her from behind thick glasses. She reached out and gave Corrine a hug. "You have grown, *jah?*"

Corrine shrugged her shoulders. "I guess so. *Daed* says I eat like I have a hollow leg."

Ella smiled. "Well, I missed you while I was gone." She gave her sister another squeeze.

Corrine gave her a curious look. "If you missed us, why didn't you ever come home? We all prayed for you to come home, but you never did."

"Oh, Corrine." Ella swallowed the lump in her throat. "I wanted to come home, really I did. I thought about all of you every day and I never stopped loving all of you and wishing I could be with you."

"People in the community still talk about you." Corrine made a face. "Kids at school say mean things."

She looked her little sister in the eye. "What do they say?" Ella was fairly certain she knew what people said, but it irritated her to no end that people would say such unkind things to members of her family.

Corrine shrugged and glanced away. "Oh, just the usual things. They say you killed Silas and Caleb Wyse. Of course I don't believe them, but they say it none the less."

Ella crouched to her sister's level. "I was driving the car that hit their buggy, *jah,* but it was an accident. If I could go back in time and prevent the accident from happening, I would."

"I know." Corrine nodded solemnly. "I told them you wouldn't intentionally hurt someone."

"*Danke,* Corrine." She hugged her sister tightly. "You don't know how much it means to me to hear you say that."

Corrine looked up at her. "Do you want to go see Susan now? I'm sure she wants to see you. She has been so sad since Isaac passed away."

"I imagine she has." Ella walked over to the stairs leading to the second floor. "She is going to need a lot of help to get through this difficult time and could use our prayers right now, don't you think?"

Corrine nodded. "I'm going to my room to pray for her right now."

Ella smiled softly. Her little sister had become a thoughtful young woman. "I think that is a wonderful idea."

She took a deep breath, oblivious to the curious stares from the other people in the room. Each of them wondering if she had finally returned home for good. She was in her own little world as she said a scripture about the Lord's guidance. After a moment, she placed one foot on the bottom stair and began to climb.

You will guide me with Your counsel, and afterward receive me to honor and glory.

Chapter Three

Susan sat propped up in one of the twin beds in Ella's childhood room. She smoothed her hands over the large mound of her stomach and smiled through her tears.

"How are you?" Ella whispered as she crossed the room to hug her longtime friend.

"I would say *gut,* but I would be lying." Susan gave her a tight squeeze. "I keep hoping I will wake up and this will all be a bad dream. I know it isn't our place to question, but I keep asking, why? First Caleb was taken and now my beloved Isaac."

"God has a plan," Ella murmured, although she was beginning to have doubts herself. "You just need to trust in Him."

"Well, I'm not sure I like God's plan." Susan wiped her eyes with the corner of the bed sheet. She placed her hand protectively on her stomach. "What am I going to do? I can't raise two *bopplies* on my own."

Ella looked her friend in the eye. "You are a capable and strong woman who is well equipped to raise these babies. You will be a *gut* mother, Susan. You have to believe that."

Anguish twisted Susan's delicate features. "Where will I stay? I won't be able to stay in the rental house for much longer. Not without an income. "

"You can stay here," Ella said, knowing as soon as the words left her mouth that it was the right thing to say. Her parents would gladly open their home to Isaac's widow. "I'm sure my parents wouldn't mind. We will always be your family."

Susan shook her head. "*Nee.* There are too many bad memories here. I need to move someplace where I can make new memories. *Gut* memories."

Ella winced. She knew that some of those bad memories had been caused by her and the knowledge of that seared her to her very soul.

Susan gave a ghost of a smile. "That is why I am thinking about moving to Kentucky to live with my *bruder* and his wife. My parents moved there last fall, so I will have a lot of family around me."

"Oh, Susan." Ella gave her a hug, noting how frail she seemed despite her advanced pregnancy. "I wish you would stay, but I can understand if you decide to leave."

"You do?"

She nodded. "My parents will be disappointed, but I know they will understand. I'm sure your mother will be a big help with the *bopplies.*"

Susan crossed her arms and did her best to frown. "And why has it taken you so long to come home? After the accident you forgot about your family and friends and disappeared into the *Englisch* world."

Ella sighed. "It was just easier to leave. *Mamm* and *Daed* were so disappointed in me. I thought Noah hated me and I didn't want to live here without him."

"Have you seen him?"

Ella thought about her former beau with the dark hair and blue eyes. A man who at this very moment, was downstairs paying his respects to a fallen friend. *"Jah,* I have. He looks good."

Susan arched her brows. "That's all you have to say? You see Noah Wyse for the first time in years and all you can say is that he looks *gut?*"

"What do you expect me to say?" Ella wished they would discuss something other than Noah Wyse. "It was awkward seeing him and I don't wish to repeat the experience any time soon."

Susan shook her head in disbelief.

Ella thought about how her heart had raced when she looked into Noah's handsome face and made a vow to have as little interaction with him as possible in the future.

Susan gave a faint smile. "You still aren't a very *gut* liar, my friend. I can tell you still care about Noah Wyse."

Ella walked over to the window. Down below, Noah was helping his mother, Luke and Megan into the buggy. As if he sensed her scrutiny, he raised his head. A small gasp escaped her lips when their gazes locked and held.

Noah gave a brief nod before turning and climbing into the buggy.

Ella watched until the buggy was out of sight, and then turned to meet Susan's speculative gaze. "Of course I still care about Noah. I will always have feelings for him, but it is obvious he has moved on with his life and I intend to do the same."

Susan nodded. "*Jah,* he has been through a lot with his wife's death and raising a son on his own. He is currently dating Megan Zehr, but I know he still cares about you."

Ella sighed. "Noah and Megan would be a good match. They both have been left alone with young children to raise."

"Maybe," Susan hesitated, "but Noah never failed to ask Isaac if he had any current news about you."

This was news to Ella. "Isaac didn't mention Noah the last time he paid me a visit." Her eyes filled with tears as she thought about her brother. "I can't believe he is gone."

Susan sniffled as fresh tears began to fall. "Isaac was so excited about the *bopplies.* He couldn't wait for them to be born."

"He would have been a wonderful father." Ella knew her brother had always wanted children and it pained her to know that he wouldn't be here for their arrival.

"*Jah,* he would have." Susan agreed. She smoothed the quilt around her and took a deep breath. "After Caleb's death, I didn't want to go on living, but Isaac mended the pieces of my shattered heart. He gave me hope for the future and now everything is gone."

"Not everything." Ella blinked back tears. "You have the precious gift of the *bopplies.*"

Susan nodded. "*Jah*. I don't know what I would do without them. The thought of seeing their sweet faces soon is the only thing that keeps me alive."

Ella hugged her friend. "Please don't say such things. There will be a lot of wonderful days in your future. You can't see it now, but God will restore happiness to your life. You just have to have faith."

"I pray constantly," Susan whispered, "but sometimes I don't think God hears my prayers."

"Oh, Susan." Ella's heart ached. "You mustn't say such things. Of course God hears your prayers. He watches over all of us."

Susan wiped away her tears. "I'm losing my faith, Ella, and it scares me. How could God take both Caleb and Isaac away from me?"

Fear snaked up Ella's spine. She prayed the Lord would help her find the right words to say to her friend. Words that would bring comfort in this dark time. "They both died in accidents, Susan. God didn't take them from you."

"*Jah.* Everyone is telling me it was God's will," bitterness dripped from Susan's words. "But how can His will be to take such a *gut* a man as Isaac?"

Ella wasn't sure what to say to her friend. She too questioned God's decision not spare Isaac's life, but at the moment that was the last thing Susan needed to hear. "Maybe you need to speak with Bishop Burkholder," Ella suggested. "He might be able to counsel you during this difficult time."

"I have." Susan's tone was flat. She wearily closed her eyes, but then opened them. "He was kind enough to stop by the night Isaac was killed."

Ella patted her friend's shoulder.

Susan clung to her. "I do believe tomorrow is going to be the saddest day of my life. How will I survive putting my Isaac in the ground?"

"The Lord will be with you," Ella whispered. Snow began to fall outside the window as she thought about a passage in Psalms.

He heals the brokenhearted and binds up their wounds.

Chapter Four

The day of Isaac's funeral dawned dark and cold. Ella shivered as she sat in her parents' buggy and watched as the wagon carrying her brother's wooden coffin slowly made its way to the small cemetery on the hill.

The wind moaned through the trees lining the road; their bare branches clacking in the increasing gale. A storm was brewing and the forecast called for heavy snow, but it didn't stop the numerous mourners as the members of the community prepared to bury one of their own.

Ella prayed for strength as the solemn procession arrived at the final destination. Climbing down from the buggy, she followed her parents down the narrow path leading to the back of the cemetery.

A large crowd had gathered. The members of the close knit community were here to say their final farewell to a man who had been a husband, a son, a brother, and a friend.

Bishop Burkholder cleared his throat and began to quote from scripture. The comforting words provided solace to their aching souls and healed their wounded hearts.

A fierce winter wind snaked around the marker stones and froze the mourners clustered in small groups around the grave, drowning out the Bishop's words and muffling the sobs of a woman who felt as if she had lost it all.

Ella glanced at Susan. She stood, supported on either side by her parents, her face drawn and pale. Her shoulders shook as she cried. Her mother whispered something in her ear and Susan straightened as she wiped away her tears, placing a hand on her stomach as if to shield the unborn babes from the harshness of the day.

Ella thought about her brother and how unfair life could be. He would never have the chance to see his children born or watch proudly as they grew to become active members in the community. Instead, he was being placed in the cold, hard ground.

She looked out over the crowd. A little further back stood the driver of the semi and his wife. Grief etched the man's features and was evident in the sagging of his shoulders.

Ella looked in the other direction, across the cemetery to where Silas and Caleb Wyse's graves lay underneath a blanket of snow. It was hard to believe six years had passed since they had been laid to rest. How different life might have been if she had never taken the car out that fateful night.

Her careless actions had changed the course of so many lives.

Ella faced forward once again and met Noah's steady gaze. He gave a brief nod as if privy to her thoughts and then turned away.

She knew that for Noah, the pain would be doubly sharp. Somewhere in this cemetery was the final resting place of the woman he had loved, married and pledged to spend the rest of his life protecting.

Her heart ached for his pain.

To her right, stood her mother and father as well as Holly, Faith and Corrine. Pain etched her parent's eyes as they watched their only son being lowered into the ground. Her mother muffled a sob and took a step forward, only to be pulled back.

Sadness threatened to overwhelm her. Ella turned, and with stumbling steps, walked through the snow toward the faint path leading to the line of buggies. Her cousin, Katie, Uncle Melvin and Aunt Ada's daughter, reached out to touch her arm as she walked past. She and Katie had always been close, but Ella shook her head and kept on walking.

Ella hesitated at her parent's buggy and debated about seeking shelter within. It was only a couple of miles to her parent's farm. Surely she could manage walking that short of a distance. With a sigh, she wrapped her coat tighter around her and decided to walk home. Lost in thought, she didn't hear the buggy as it pulled alongside.

"Ella?" The familiar deep voice halted her in her tracks. She would have known it anywhere.

"Do you need a ride home?" Noah climbed down from the buggy and walked to her side. Once there, he regarded her with a mixture of disapproval and concern.

Ella forced herself to meet his troubled gaze. If she was going to live in LaGrange County she needed to get use to running into Noah Wyse. "*Nee.* I'm fine. *Danke* for offering."

Noah sighed. "Don't be silly. It is far too cold for you to walk home. I can take you home before I drop off Megan."

Ella looked toward the buggy where Megan Zehr sat, regarding her with a tense smile.

"*Nee.* I don't want to be a bother. I'm fine. A little cold won't hurt me."

"Ella," Noah said through gritted teeth. "Please get in the buggy." He held out his hand and then sighed when she refused to take it.

The cold wind tore at their clothing and dashed the icy snowflakes in the air against their cheeks. The smartest thing to do would be to accept his offer, but she couldn't overcome her pride.

Ella lifted chin. "I don't want to cause problems for you and your girlfriend."

A muscle jumped in Noah's jaw. He leaned forward until his lips were close to her ear. "She isn't my girlfriend," he growled. "We're just friends."

Several buggies rolled by, the occupants craning their necks to observe the two figures standing at the side of the road.

Ella turned to look out over the field, her back facing any onlookers. "It's okay if she is your girlfriend. I will understand."

Noah shook his head at her stubbornness. "Ella, this isn't the time nor the place to be having this conversation. *Please* get in the buggy so I can take you home."

"Fine." Ella grasped his outstretched hand and allowed him to help her into the buggy. "I will allow you to take me home, but only because we are causing a scene. And you must agree to take Megan home first. She has small children waiting for her."

"Anything to get you out of this cold." Noah climbed in beside her.

Megan nodded a greeting, but otherwise remained silent as they traveled the few miles to her home. A short time later, they pulled up in front of a neat, single story home. Empty flower beds lined the short walkway and Ella knew that in the summer, they would be filled with an array of blooming flowers.

A green sedan was parked in the drive.

As if noticing the direction of her gaze, Megan gave an explanation. "My neighbor offered to watch my children so I could attend your brother's funeral."

"*Danke,* for going to all the trouble." Ella could sense a coolness from the other woman. A barely detectable undercurrent of dislike as she fought to remain polite.

Megan gave a brief nod. "It was no trouble. Your brother was a *gut* friend to everyone and will be sorely missed in the community." She smiled sadly. "Please tell Susan I will drop by to see her sometime in the next few days. I know how difficult the next few months will be for her."

"I will tell her," Ella said, remembering that Megan had suffered a loss recently as well.

Noah exited the buggy and walked around to assist Megan. She gave a smile that barely lifted her lips before stepping down.

Ella sighed as she watched Noah walk Megan to her door. Despite Noah's assurances that he and Megan were only friends, anyone with eyes could see otherwise. They were clearly a couple and she had no business interfering, no matter what her broken heart wanted.

"She still means a lot to you," Megan said as they stepped up onto the porch.

Noah looked away, but didn't deny the truth in her words. "I will always care for Ella, but circumstances have changed. We aren't the naïve children we were six years ago."

Megan smiled sadly. "Maybe not, but that doesn't mean you couldn't have a future together."

Noah gave her a quick hug. "You are a *gut* friend, Megan."

Megan wiped away a tear as she watched Noah walk back to the buggy. She knew that no matter how much she prayed, the only thing she and Noah would ever be, was friends.

God had plans for her future. In time he would bring someone into her life who would be a wonderful partner to her and a father to her children. But she now knew that Noah Wyse wasn't that man.

Noah climbed back into the buggy and put it in motion. Silence reigned as they headed down the quiet country road.

Ella attempted to break the silence that was threatening to suffocate her. "How is your sister, Audry?"

"She's fine," Noah answered without taking his eyes off the road. "She has her hands full with all of her children, but she seems happy."

"Good," Ella said, and meant it. She and Audry had been close growing up and it would be wonderful to see her again.

"We need to talk, Ella." Noah's voice was rough with emotion as he glanced in her direction. "We left a lot of things unsaid six years ago."

"*Jah.* We did." Her teeth worried her lower lip. She didn't know if she wanted to hear what he had to say.

Noah took a deep breath and then let it out. "After you left, I searched for you."

Ella glanced sideways at him. This was a surprise. After the accident she had been certain he hated her. "I thought you were angry. You didn't speak to me at your father and *bruder's* funeral. Nor did you seek me out in the following weeks."

Noah sighed. "I'm not angry, at least not anymore. A little confused, but not angry." He speared her with his dark, blue gaze. "It was God's will. *Jah*?"

Ella arched her brows in surprise. "You can't possibly believe that?"

"I have to, Ella," he said as he steered the buggy onto the road leading to her parents' farm. "For my own sanity I have to believe the entire horrible incident was God's plan. Just like Rebecca's death was a part of his plan. How can I think otherwise?"

She felt tears beginning to form. "After that night, I was hurt and confused. I had trouble coming to grips with what I had done. So, I decided to leave. I wanted to go someplace where people knew nothing of the accident and wouldn't greet me with whispers and cold stares."

Noah's voice was a low growl. "You didn't give us a chance to salvage our relationship. You gave up on me. You gave up on us."

"How could I not?" Ella didn't dare look at the man who had once meant so much to her.

"I pestered your parents for months trying to find out where you had gone, but they said they didn't know."

She nodded. "They told the truth. I didn't contact them for a couple of years. Selfish, I know, but I was afraid they would try to talk me into coming home before I was ready."

Noah pulled the buggy over to the side of the road and raised his hand to caress her cheek, but stopped, letting it fall back into his lap.

Ella pretended not to notice.

"I prayed for you." Noah's voice was a soft whisper in the confines of the buggy. "I prayed for us."

"You did?"

"Jah." He nodded. "Every night before I went sleep I said a prayer asking God to bring you back to me, but after waiting six months, I gave up."

"You gave up?"

Noah was silent for a moment. *"Jah,* after so much time had passed and you hadn't returned, I moved to Maine and stayed with my Aunt and Uncle for a couple of years."

"But you came back," Ella said, stating the obvious.

"I did, yes, but only after I heard through Isaac that your parents had located you in West Lafayette on Purdue's campus. So, I decided to move back home and pray that God would work on your heart and return you to where you belonged."

"I didn't come back." Her whisper floated between them. "After I graduated I moved to Indianapolis."

He nodded as if he had been well aware where she had been living the past two years. "*Jah,* well, after a time I began dating Rebecca Lapp. We married that fall and our son was born the following August." He gave a smile that didn't quite reach his eyes.

Ella smiled softly. "Luke is wonderful. I'm sure you must be proud."

Noah nodded. "I know that pride is a sin, but I can't help but feel blessed to be his father."

Ella looked into is eyes. "Noah, I'm...I'm sorry for all of the hurt you have suffered."

He turned away. "Sometimes God know what's best."

"And what do you think is best?" She wasn't sure she wanted to hear the answer to her question, but she had to ask.

Noah shrugged. "I don't know what to think." He pulled the buggy back onto the road and was quiet for a few moments. At last he spoke. "I would like the chance to be your friend. If we can't be anything else, we can at least be friends, *jah?*"

Ella didn't want to be just friends, but knew she had no right asking for anything more. She had given up the right to be more than just friends the day she had packed her bags and taken a bus south. "*Jah,* we will always be friends," she whispered.

A short time later, they pulled up in front of her parent's house. A few buggies still lined the drive, but it looked as if the majority of the people had gone home to tend to little ones and chores.

She grasped Noah's large, warm hand as he helped her down from the buggy, then hastily took a step back. "Do you want to come inside? I'm sure we have plenty to eat."

He shook his head. "*Nee.* I need to get home. Luke will be waiting." He looked away as if fighting an internal battle, then faced her.

"Would you like to go for a buggy ride tomorrow evening, weather permitting that is?"

Ella could only stare at him in shock. "I thought you wanted to be just friends?"

He shifted on his feet. "*Jah,* I do, but I also would like to talk with you more. We have a lot of catching up to do, don't you agree?"

"*Jah,*" she said in a rush before he could change his mind. "I would love to go with you."

Noah's expression was serious. "We can only be friends, Ella. That is what I'm offering."

Ella looked out over the frozen landscape as she searched for the words to say. "That's fine," she said, her words sounding false even to her own ears. "One can never have too many friends."

Noah looked relieved. "*Gut.* I will stop by after dinner." He turned to leave, but stopped.

"Please tell your *daed* I will be here early in the morning for work."

Startled, Ella remembered that Noah worked in her father's furniture shop. The business had been started by her grandfather Graber and the elderly man still spent a couple of hours a day working alongside his son. Isaac had worked in the shop as well, but now they would need to find a replacement.

A lump formed in her throat. "I will," she whispered at his retreating back.

Snowflakes began to fall, spiraling gently to the ground. Ella walked slowly to the house as she pondered the situation with Noah. Could she ever be content to just be friends with a man who would have been her husband if life had gone differently? She began to silently pray, asking for the Lord's help and was startled when a s

quickly came to mind.

   I sought the Lord, and he heard me, And

delivered me from all my fears.

Chapter Five

Ella awoke to bright sunlight streaming through her bedroom window. With bleary eyes she sat up in bed and peered at the travel clock on the nightstand and was shocked to see it was already past ten o'clock. She had slept far longer than intended. Her family would think she had become lazy during the years she had been gone.

Hastily scrambling out of bed, Ella picked up a dress, apron, and *kapp* someone must have placed on a chair while she was sleeping. Looking closer, Ella recognized the green dress as being one she had left behind.

She looked toward her suitcase which contained her worn jeans and comfortable tops and decided against them. If only for today, she would wear the clothes that would make her family the most comfortable in her presence.

Ella thought about the recent events and the lingering sadness that would permeate their existence until time and prayer began to heal the pain Isaac's death had wrought. She knelt by the bed and began to pray, asking the Lord to heal their broken hearts and bring peace to the family once again.

Ella finished her prayers and rose. She existed the room and padded quickly down the hall to take a shower.

It was almost eleven by the time she entered the kitchen. Her mother was busy taking loaves of fresh bread out of the oven. She turned and smiled warmly. *"Guder mariye."*

"Good morning, *Mamm.*" Ella poured herself a cup of coffee and sat down at the table next to her grandmother who was nursing a cup of coffee of her own.

Her grandmother gave her a pat on the knee as she had so often over the years and smiled. "Happy to have you join us this morning, granddaughter."

Ella ducked her head in embarrassment. Her grandmother rose at the break of dawn every day and would have already been up for hours. "I guess I overslept a little."

Her grandmother winked. "Don't worry. It happens to all of us."

Ella looked toward her sisters, Holly and Faith, who were busy stirring up double batches of chocolate whoopie pies. She had missed the delicious treats over the years, but hadn't had the heart to bake a batch just for herself.

Her mother pulled a rasher of bacon and a carton of eggs out of the refrigerator. "What would you like to eat this morning?"

"Please don't bother, *Mamm*," Ella said, feeling guilty that her mother felt the need to cater to her. "I usually don't eat breakfast. Besides, it's almost lunchtime."

Her mother gave a look of disapproval, but put the items back in the refrigerator. "You need to eat more, Ella. You've gotten too skinny."

Faith snorted.

Holly gave her a poke in the ribs then turned to Ella. "Guess who stopped by to speak to you this morning?"

Ella sat her coffee mug down with a clunk. Surely she wasn't talking about Noah? Maybe he had changed his mind about their outing this evening.

Holly smiled. "Noah was very eager to speak with you. He seemed to be disappointed when I told him you weren't up yet."

"*Jah,*" Faith rolled her eyes. "It looks as if you have caught Noah's eye again. Megan Zehr isn't going to be happy."

Faith and Holly both giggled, earning them a stern look from *mamm.*

"Girls!" *Mamm* clapped her hands. "Enough of this gossip. You both know Noah stopped in before work to return a cake pan his mother had borrowed. Now there is plenty of work for you to finish before tomorrows' bake sale, but if you need me to find you more, I will be happy to oblige."

Ella was eager to change the conversation. The last thing she wanted to talk about with her family was Noah Wyse and why he wished to speak to her. "What bake sale?"

Her mother poured herself a cup of *kaffi* and sat down across from her. "The community has decided to hold a bake sale for Susan to help her with her expenses."

"How is Susan?" Ella pictured her sister-in-law the way she had looked at the funeral and knew that she must be feeling lost and alone.

Mamm sighed. "She is still distraught, but she is determined to be strong for the *bopplies*. Her brother and his wife returned to Kentucky this morning, but her father and mother are staying to help her pack."

"She hasn't changed her mind about moving?"

"*Nee,* she hasn't," *Mamm* said sadly. "Amos Yoder owns the house she is renting and has been kind enough to let her out of the lease."

Ella had passed the quaint house plenty of times. At one point, she and Noah had discussed purchasing the property, but that had been long ago. She willed away the memories of a time long past. "Surely her doctor doesn't approve of her traveling?"

"*Nee*," *Mamm* sighed, "but I suspect Susan will do what she wants and no one will hold it against her after all she's been through."

Ella stared into her coffee cup. She didn't want Susan to leave, but she couldn't blame her for wanting to put distance between herself and the place where she had experienced so much pain.

"Ach, look at the time." Her mother jumped to her feet. "I need to get food ready for *meddaagesse.* It won't be long before the men come in to eat."

Holly checked the pantry and the refrigerator. "I'm sure we have plenty of food left over from the many dishes brought by our friends and neighbors. We will have plenty to eat for lunch."

Their mother shook her head. "*Nee.* I will fix something." She grabbed a couple of loaves of Italian bread, a block of cheddar cheese, provolone cheese and Swiss cheese. "I think I will make grilled cheese and tomato soup. It is a cold day, the *menner* will want something hot to eat."

Faith walked over and gave Ella a nudge. "Noah usually eats lunch with us," she whispered.

Ella gasped and rushed from the room to freshen up, followed by her sisters' laughter. By the time she returned, the men were already seated at the table.

The room was quiet as she halted in the kitchen doorway, her eyes seeking out Noah. She flushed when she met his steady gaze and quickly looked away when he gave her a lopsided smile.

"You look nice," he murmured.

"*Danke,*" she whispered, suddenly becoming tongue tied. Why did this man have the ability to make her feel discombobulated?

"*Jah*," her father agreed, looking in Ella's direction. "Its *gut* to see you dressing properly again." He gave her a smile of approval before lowering his head to lead the silent blessing.

The meal passed quickly, with the women discussing the upcoming bake sale and the men talking about orders they needed to complete. It wasn't until their father mentioned finding a replacement for Isaac that the conversation came to a halt.

Mamm gave a choked sob, lowering her head.

"Now, Gretta." Their father rose to give their mother a comforting hug. "No one will ever replace Isaac in our hearts, but we need to fill his position in the shop. We have several orders waiting to be completed and need to find a qualified person quickly."

Mamm sniffled. *"Jah,* Abram. I know what you say is true, but please don't fault me for grieving our *sohn.*"

Grandfather Graber cleared his throat. "Ethan Miller has expressed interest in the position. From what I've seen, he does *gut* work."

Abram nodded. "We will discuss this back at the shop."

The men rose as one and quietly filed out the door.

Ella stared after Noah, hoping he would give her one last glance, but he appeared to be deeply engrossed in conversation with her father. She sighed and turned back to the table, only to find her mother, grandmother and sisters eyeing her speculatively.

Her mother motioned for her sisters to leave the room. They groaned, but filed out quietly.

Holly gave her an encouraging smile as she walked past. "Good luck," she whispered.

Ella sat rooted to her chair. She had a good idea what was to be the topic of conversation and braced herself to receive her mother's advice.

Her mother shook her head. "Noah Wyse is a good man who has been through a lot over the past few years." She waited patiently for Ella to respond, but after receiving none, continued. "He has had to come to terms with not only the death of his father and twin brother, but the death of his young wife as well."

Ella sighed. "We're just friends. We haven't seen each other in years, so I don't expect for our relationship to pick up where it left off. He is a father now."

Her mother gave her a serious look. "*Jah,* and it would be wise for you to remember that. Noah has a young *sohn* and doesn't need to get involved with someone who may or may not stay in our community."

Her mother's words stung. Ella searched for the words that would alleviate her mother's concern. "But…"

Mamm waved away her protests. "I know how much you cared for Noah Wyse and him for you, but the accident changed a few things. Noah lost both is father and twin brother and even though I know he wouldn't consciously blame you, there has to be some underlying resentment."

"He claims there isn't," Ella said softly.

Mamm looked her straight in the eye. "You are an adult, and it isn't my place to tell you what to do in your relationships, but please be careful. Noah is a wonderful man and would make a *gut* husband, but I'm not sure if he is the right man for you."

"We are just friends." Ella repeated. "He doesn't want to be anything more." She looked to her grandmother for support, but found that she had slipped out of the room.

Ella rose to her feet.

"Ella," her mother pleaded, "I have eyes. He still has feelings for you."

"And I for him." Ella sat back down at the table, wishing she were anywhere, but here. She had lived on her own for six years, but somehow in this house she still felt like a child.

Her mother gave her a serious look. "Noah has been courting Megan Zehr for the past few months. Everyone expects them to announce their plans to wed next fall." Her mother sighed. "It is a relationship that might be the best for the both of them."

Ella was startled even though she knew her mother's words had to be true. Hadn't she witnessed the couple's close bond just yesterday? "Noah asked if he could stop by tonight after dinner. He wants to talk to me, but only as a friend."

Her mother sighed and shook her head. "Just be careful, daughter."

"I will." Ella would be careful, but she wasn't sure she could guard her heart. Her dreams last night had been filled with a dark haired man with blue eyes. She sighed. No, there wasn't any point in guarding her heart. She had given it to Noah Wyse long ago and that was where it remained.

Chapter Six

Ella helped her mother and sisters put away the remaining supper dishes and tidy up the kitchen. She was surprised at how much she had missed the simple chore and the feeling of togetherness spending time with her family always gave.

A blanket of peace had settled over the house with the setting of the sun and she found herself smiling at the familiar tranquility. She had taken her peaceful life for granted when she lived here and had gone out of her way to bend rules and seek excitement. Now she was happy as she immersed herself in the community's slower pace.

Ella worried about her grandparents as she dried the last dish and placed it in the cupboard.

Her grandmother seemed as chipper as ever, but her grandfather had aged significantly in the years since she had been gone. After supper they had retired to their quarters. A small house built onto the main house.

Her attention turned to Corrine. She couldn't get over how much her little sister had grown over the past few years. Corrine sat in a rocking chair by the wood stove, working on a quilting square. A slight frown marred her forehead as she concentrated on her stitches.

Ella walked over to admire her sister's work. "It's very pretty, Corrine. You are a *gut* quilter."

Corrine looked up at her in surprise. "I am not as good a quilter as you. My stitches aren't as straight as yours."

"Ach, *nee.*" Ella waved away the compliment. "I haven't quilted in a long time."

"Why not?" Holly finished wiping the counter and sat down at the table with a sigh. "You use to love to quilt."

Ella shrugged. "I've been too busy, I guess." Her life in Indianapolis had been fast paced. She had often worked from the wee hours of the morning straight through until late at night on lesson plans. Truth be told, she hadn't minded. She had had no special person to share her free time.

She poured herself a cup of coffee and sat down at the table. "Faith sure took off like a shot." She noted her younger sister's hasty departure from the kitchen.

Her mother smiled softly. "You were the same way when you were that age. I just hope..." *Mamm's* voice trailed off.

"What? That she doesn't turn out like me?" Ella whispered, as tears threatened. "That she doesn't decide to learn to drive and plow into a buggy on a dark, rainy night killing her boyfriend's brother and *daed*?"

"Oh, Ella." Her mother gave her a hug. "That isn't what I meant. Your father and I don't approve of her spending so much time with her *Englisch* friends."

"That's true." Her father walked into the room. "We don't approve. But I trust God to watch out for our Faith just like he watched out for Ella while she was away from us." He gave Ella's shoulder a gentle squeeze as he walked past to get another piece of chocolate cream pie from the refrigerator.

"Abram, the doctor told you to watch your weight," *Mamm* cautioned.

Daed chuckled. "I am watching my weight, Gretta. The bigger my stomach gets, the better I can keep an eye on it." He placed a large wedge of pie on a plate then leaned down to kiss his wife's cheek. "You shouldn't be such a *gut* cook if you want me to be thin."

"Oh, Abram." *Mamm* smiled at his retreating back as he took his piece of pie into the parlor. "Whatever am I going to do with that man?"

They all laughed.

Ella smiled. She couldn't help but hope for a marriage like her parents' someday. Her mother was blessed with a husband who adored her and several children. The only thing keeping it from being perfect was the absence of Isaac.

"A buggy just pulled up," Holly announced as she peered out the kitchen window. "Is that Noah?"

Ella shot to her feet and grabbed her coat. She hoped to escape the house quickly to avoid any more questions. "I should be home in a couple of hours."

Her mother shook her head. "I know you are both adults, Ella, but please be careful. It wouldn't be fair to Noah to renew your friendship if you are just going to turn around and leave."

"I know, *Mamm.*" Ella glanced out the window at the buggy. Her heart leapt with excitement as she watched Noah climb down. "We're just going to talk. I promise."

Her mother nodded. "I trust you, Ella, but sometimes emotions tend to take over."

Ella gave her mother a hug. "I'll be careful."

"Megan will be crushed if she finds out Noah was here." Holly plopped down in a chair with a cup of coffee. "She has been sniffing around Noah for the past year."

"Holly," *Mamm* frowned. "Women don't sniff after men. I'm sure it has been a difficult time for Megan since her husband past away. It can't be easy raising two small children alone."

"Sorry, *Mamm*," Holly murmured.

Ella slipped out the kitchen door before Noah could knock. A cold breeze brushed her skin and she silently prayed for guidance as she walked toward the waiting buggy.

Should she follow her heart? Or would following her heart crush another woman's hopes and dreams? Her only answer was the wind as it whistled through the bare branches of the maple trees.

Chapter Seven

Noah met her with a big smile. "I've been looking forward to this all day." He helped her into the buggy then climbed in beside her.

Ella turned and was startled to find herself staring into Luke's big blue eyes. He sat in the back wrapped in a warm blanket. She smiled at the little boy and her heart melted when she was rewarded with a shy grin. "I didn't expect you to bring your son."

Noah arched his brows and then shook his head. "*Jah,* well, I'm a father now," he said as if explaining the situation to a small child. "My time isn't my own." Noah passed her a lap blanket and then set the buggy in motion.

Ella snuggled under the blanket Noah provided and watched his strong hands on the reins. She hadn't realized how much she had missed the long rides they use to take in his buggy several times a week.

Noah pulled the buggy out onto the road and they rode in silence for about a mile. A short time later, he pulled into the driveway of an empty farmhouse.

Ella leaned forward on the bench and surveyed the landscape around her. It had begun to snow again, large flakes danced and whirled around the buggy before falling to the ground. She studied the property. She recognized the house as one that had been owned by Leroy and Waneta Fisher before they moved to Canada to be with their grown children. She had always loved the place with its well-tended lawn and large oak trees.

Noah turned to look at her. "Well, what do you think?"

"About what?" Ella wasn't sure why he had brought her here. They couldn't possibly be visiting, because the house had been empty for a good many years.

Noah grinned, twin dimples flashing in his cheeks. "What do you think about the house?"

She gazed at the house in the fading light. It was a two-story farmhouse with a wrap-around porch. A large barn with peeling paint stood off to the right. It was a wonderful property, but she couldn't fathom why they were sitting in its driveway on such a cold, dark night.

"It's nice," Ella said as she studied his face trying to gage his intent. "It would be a *gut* place for a family."

Noah nodded. "It is nice," he agreed.

"Noah," she said softly. "Surely you didn't bring me here so we could discuss the merits of the property?"

He removed his hat and ran a hand through his hair causing it to stand on end. "I put an offer on the property today after I got off work."

Ella stared at him in shock. "I hope your decision didn't have anything to do with me?" the words were out of her mouth before she could stop them. It was a slight untruth, but she hoped the Lord would forgive her.

Noah laughed as if she had said something funny and shook his head. "*Nee.* I have considered buying this property for months now. Luke is getting older and while it has been nice living at my mother's, it is time we have a place of our own. Eventually I would like to have a horse farm, but that is a few years down the road."

"A horse farm?" Ella looked at him in surprise, then laughed. "Why would you want to have a horse farm?"

Noah chuckled. "Don't laugh. I have wanted to raise horses since I was a boy and visited my Uncle and Aunt's farm in Missouri."

"I'm not laughing," Ella said, trying to put on a serious face and failing. She wrinkled her nose. "I just can't picture you raising horses, that's all."

Noah placed a hand over his heart. "I'm hurt," he said, then winked.

Ella caught her breath at his familiar boyish grin. She had missed his warm smile, but she knew he was teasing her, the way one did a close friend.

It had gotten colder. She shivered and burrowed further into her coat. She glanced in the back of the buggy and found that Luke was sound asleep. A dark curl had tumbled over his forehead and she longed to sweep it away and place a motherly kiss on his sweet brow.

"Cold?" Noah reached behind him and pulled a second blanket out of the back. He then turned and wrapped another blanket around his sleeping son.

"*Danke*." Ella took the blanket from his hands, grateful for the added warmth. "What about you? Aren't you cold?"

"*Nee.*" He shook his head. "The cold doesn't bother me much."

Ella looked at a large oak tree in the front yard. The branches were thick and wide and would be an excellent spot for picnics during the warm summer months. "That tree would be the perfect place to hang a tire swing for Luke, don't you think?"

Noah leaned over to see where she was pointing. "*Jah,* it would make a fine place for a swing." He grinned. "I seem to recall seeing the Fisher's grandchildren swinging from that very tree a time or two."

Ella wrinkled her brow. "So, you've had your eye on this property for months?" She knew Noah would have taken the time to think through his decision, carefully weighing the pros and cons.

Noah scratched his bearded chin. "Years, really. After we were married, Rebecca and I lived with my mother so we could save money for a property of our own. This is one of the properties we considered buying." Noah's expression saddened and he turned away.

"I'm sorry," Ella whispered, "it must be difficult without her."

Noah nodded and sighed heavily. "Rebecca brought such joy to my life after…" He left the sentence unfinished, but they both knew what he failed to say. He turned back to face her. "She was a *gut* wife and mother," he said firmly, as if he needed to somehow convince her of the fact.

They sat in silence for a few minutes before Noah asked, "What about you? Surely after all these years you have someone special in your life?"

"*Nee,*" Ella shook her head. "I haven't dated much." She hadn't dated at all since she left, but she kept that information to herself.

He looked at her in surprise. "There's no one waiting for you back in Indianapolis?"

"*Nee,* there isn't."

Noah looked relieved, but quickly changed the subject. "Megan loves this property," he said as if he knew by mentioning the other woman's name it would break the tension between them. "She never fails to mention it every time we drive past."

Ella struggled to hide her disappointment. He had thought about purchasing the property while he had been courting Megan. She couldn't help but feel he had planned a future with the widow. This property would be the perfect place to raise Luke as well as Megan's two children.

She willed away her bitterness and smiled. "I'm happy for you. I know you've wanted your own property for a long time. This would be a wonderful place for you to raise Luke."

"*Danke,* Ella." Noah smiled. "It means a lot to me to hear you say that. I've wanted my own farm since I was a boy, but I never thought it would actually happen." He hesitated. "I like working in your family's furniture business, but someday I want to have a business of my own."

"I'm sure Megan will be thrilled with your decision." The words sprung forth from her mouth as if they had a life of their own. Oh, how she wished she could take the offending sentence back.

"Ella," Noah growled, a hint of anger flashing in his eyes. "I told you, Megan and I are just friends. I can't believe you thought my putting an offer on this place had anything to do with her. My actions have to do with my son and what is best for him and *nothing* to do with Megan Zehr."

"Well, what else am I to think?" Ella shrugged, knowing she had no right to speak to Noah in this manner, but found was unable to stop herself. "According to Holly you have been dating Megan for months and everyone expects the two of you to announce your intent to marry in the fall. This would be a wonderful place for your son as well as Megan and her children."

Noah sighed and shook his head as if he regretted his decision to bring her here. "Megan and I courted for a short time, that is true, but we ended our relationship a couple of months ago. We both decided we would be better off as friends."

Ella secretly wondered if he had bothered to inform Megan of this arrangement, but kept it to herself. "This is a lovely place, Noah," she said in an attempt to undo the damage she had caused. "I hope your offer is accepted."

"*Danke.*" He leaned closer. "You are the first person I've told."

Her heart fluttered.

"I've missed you, Ella." Noah's voice was low and husky. "You were my best friend."

"You were my best friend too," she said, remembering all of the fun and laughter they had shared before her selfish actions had taken away the good times and left only pain.

He hesitated. "After Rebecca died it felt as if my entire world had come to an end. The only thing keeping me alive was Luke and how much he needed me." He glanced into the back at his young son and his expression softened. "It has been a difficult few years, but there have also been blessings."

Ella lowered her head in shame.

Noah turned to her. "I'm not sure if this is the right thing to do, but I would like the chance to see you again. As friends," he clarified when hope sprang in to her eyes.

Ella's voice wobbled. "I cost you two people who were very dear to you. Why on earth would you want to be my friend?"

Noah didn't argue. "Losing my *daed* was tough, but losing my twin *bruder* was far worse. I felt as if I had lost the other half of me. Sometimes I still can't believe Caleb is truly gone." He sighed. "As far as being your friend," he looked her in the eyes, "everyone needs a friend."

Tears pricked Ella's eyes. "I'm sorry for all the hurt I've caused. Your brother, Gideon, and your mother must hate me."

Noah sighed and stared out into the darkness. "No one hates you, Ella, least of all me. We were all hurt by your actions, but we've learned to forgive. Caleb and *Daed* always liked you and wouldn't want us to harbor any ill feelings."

"Danke, Noah." She blinked back tears. "Your words of forgiveness mean the world to me."

He turned away from her, wiping his eyes. *"Jah,* well, there's no use talking about the past. What's done is done."

Ella placed a hand on is arm, but he shrugged it off and picked up the reins. "We best be getting back, *jah?* I need to get home and put Luke to bed."

Hurt by his dismissal, she could only nod. In her heart she knew that even though Noah spoke about forgiveness, it would be a long time before he truly forgave. Now she needed to work on forgiving herself. She meditated on a scripture as they began the slow ride home.

Do not judge, and you will not be judged. Do not condemn, and you will not be condemned. Forgive, and you will be forgiven.

Chapter Eight

The house was dark and quiet when Ella returned. She climbed the old wooden stairs, carefully maneuvered around the squeaky stair tread halfway from the top, and eased open the bedroom door. She hoped to find Holly asleep so as to avoid any questions. She needed to think about what had transpired tonight and pray for guidance before discussing the evening with another person.

Holly sat up in bed as soon as Ella entered. "Well?" Her younger sister smiled knowingly. "How did it go?"

Ella shrugged as she changed into her nightclothes and crawled underneath the heavy quilt on the twin bed. "We talked, that's all."

Holly sighed in exasperation. "So what did the two of you talk about for all that time? There had to have been some reason he was so eager to see you."

Ella turned toward her sister. "Do you remember the old Fisher place?"

Holly gave her a puzzled look. "*Jah*, of course. When we were children we use to pretend we lived there every time we rode past. Waneta Fisher always kept such lovely flower beds."

"*Jah,* she did," Ella agreed. "I hadn't thought about that place in years until Noah took me there tonight."

Holly frowned. "Why on earth would he do that? I thought he took you on a buggy ride so the two of you could talk."

"Oh, we did," Ella reassured her. "But Noah wanted me to see the Fisher place for a special reason."

Holly's eyes sparkled with excitement. "Well, don't leave me hanging. What was the *special* reason?"

Ella debated whether or not she should say anything else, but knew she would have no peace until Holly learned the reason behind Noah's actions. "He put an offer on the property and he wanted me to be the first to know."

Holly squealed as she bounced up and down on her bed in excitement. "Oh, Ella. That's wonderful."

"*Jah*" Ella said, hoping her sister was n't getting any crazy ideas in her head. "It will be a nice place for Noah to rear his son and any future children he has if he chooses to marry again, but

I'm sure thoughts of marriage are furthest from his mind."

"Don't be so sure." Holly shook her head. "Why else would he bother to take you there? A man doesn't show a woman a property he is thinking about purchasing unless she is important to him."

Ella seriously doubted if Holly knew much about men, but she did have a point. She sat up in bed and ran a hand through her thick hair, working out the tangles while she came up with an answer.

Holly folded her arms and waited.

Ella sighed, knowing she had stalled long enough. "He said the only reason he wanted to tell me is because we use to be such *gut* friends. I haven't been back home long enough for him to develop feelings for me again."

Holly snorted. *"Jah,* and pigs fly. He didn't take you to see the property because you are his good friend, Ella."

Ella shook her head in disagreement. "Maybe. Maybe not. I still think Noah is in love with Megan."

Holly giggled. "I don't. I've seen the way he looks at you. And if he still had feelings for Megan Zehr, he would have shown her the property instead of you."

"How does he look at me?" Ella asked with baited breath.

Holly gave her an incredulous look. "Oh, please. Don't tell me you didn't notice the goo-goo eyes he was giving you yesterday?"

"Holly!" Ella was shocked. "You sound like the children I use to teach. And I seriously doubt if Noah was behaving improperly at our *bruder's* funeral!" She gave her sister a disappointed look. "To answer your question, no, I didn't notice him looking at me in any such way."

Holly shook her head in disbelief. "You must be blind, sister dear. Anyone with eyes in their head can tell he still cares for you."

Ella was uncomfortable with the direction this conversation was taking. "We shouldn't be discussing whether or not Noah Wyse still has feelings for me. It isn't proper."

Holly sighed and flopped back against her pillow. "My goodness, Ella. When did you become such a prude?"

From downstairs came the sound of knocking. Their parent's bedroom door opened and the heavy tread of their father's footsteps descended the stairs followed by the lighter footsteps of their mother.

A few minutes later their mother opened the bedroom door. "That was Susan's father," she said excitedly. "Susan is having the *bopplies.*" She turned and rushed back down the hallway.

Ella and Holly jumped to their feet and began to dress.

"Isn't it too early for the *bopplies* to be born?" Holly whispered as they made their way down the stairs and into the kitchen.

"*Jah.*" Ella nodded. "The babies are due next month but twins often arrive early."

Their mother rushed about throwing items they might need into a basket. She smiled as her daughters entered the room and began to pull on her coat. "Ella and Holly, you are to come with me. Your *daed* is staying here with Corrine."

Ella looked around the room. "What about Faith? Can't she stay with Corrine?"

Their mother frowned. "Faith is still out with her friends. She and I will have a discussion about her staying out so late when she gets home."

"Well, she is in her *rumspringa.*" Ella attempted to defend her sibling but only earned a dark look from her mother.

"There are still rules to be followed," *Mamm* said sharply as they headed out the door. "Faith needs to stop running around with her *Englisch* friends and focus on joining the church. Spending too much time in the *Englisch* world will only lead to trouble."

Ella couldn't help but feel her mother was referring to her and the trouble she had caused during her *rumspringa.* As far as her parents were concerned, the *Englisch* world had already had a bad influence on one daughter, they couldn't risk it poisoning any more of their children.

Holly gave her arm a comforting pat as they walked toward the waiting buggy. "Don't worry," she whispered. "*Mamm* and *daed* don't blame you for Faith's actions."

"*Danke,* Holly." Ella knew her sister's words were kind, but untrue. Their mother and father did think that Ella's past behavior had negatively influenced her siblings. She only hoped her current actions overshadowed her transgressions from the past.

Ella prayed on the way to Susan's house while Holly and their mother talked excitedly about the arrival of the babies. She knew in her heart God would watch over Susan and the *bopplies,* but she couldn't help but pray for Him to provide them extra protection. Susan had been through so much heartache in her young life. She deserved to have the delivery of her *bopplies* go as smoothly as possible.

It wasn't long before they were pulling into the driveway of Susan's single story house. Her father walked out of the barn to greet them. Weariness shown in his eyes and they held a hint of fear. He didn't speak, but quickly unharnessed their horse, and led him into the barn.

Ella hadn't attended a birth before. The fact that this was her brother's wife made the situation even more difficult. She took a fortifying breath of cold night air before opening the door and walking inside.

Late night shadows bathed the inside of Susan's small household. The sole light came from a kerosene lamp burning in the kitchen.

Susan's father came in from outside. He offered them a cup of coffee from the pot sitting on the stove. "I want to thank you for coming out in the cold. Susan asked for you to be here." He shifted and stared at his feet.

"There's no need to thank us." Their mother got out a large pot and began to boil water. "There is no other place we would rather be."

Susan's father nodded solemnly. "Well, *danke,* all the same," he mumbled, before leaving the room.

"I wonder how long it will take for the *bopplies* to be born?" Holly cast a worried glance in the direction of Susan's bedroom. "We could be here for hours."

Their mother gave Holly a withering look. "We are here to help, not complain."

"Sorry, *Mamm,*" Holly whispered, sounding more like a child than a woman of twenty-two. "I won't complain anymore."

"See that you don't." *Mamm* gave her daughter a hug. "I know this night will be a difficult one for all of us but our presence will be a comfort to Susan."

Susan's room was located down a short hallway. Ella could hear Susan's frantic cries and the murmur of Ruth Lapp, the local midwife, trying to comfort her. She lowered her head and began to pray for the Lord to take control of the situation and ease Susan's pain.

Susan's mother, Lizzie Troyer, exited the bedroom and joined them at the kitchen table. Dark circles were underneath her eyes and she glanced back at the room nervously. "Ruth says it won't be much longer now."

"Das gut," Mamm murmured, motioning for the other woman to take a seat. "We have been praying that Susan has an easy delivery."

The shrill cry of a newborn baby pierced the stillness of the night.

Lizzie and *Mamm* both jumped to their feet.

Ella gazed toward heaven and thanked the Lord for watching over Susan and her growing family. Tears formed in her eyes as she thought that even through the darkness that had surrounded this family over the past few days, the Lord could bring light.

"One of the *bopplies* is here," Lizzie exclaimed as she raced toward the bedroom with their mother close on her heels.

"Should we go in and see the baby?" Holly asked, half rising from her seat.

Ella shook her head. *"Nee,* the bedroom will be crowded and Susan still hasn't had the second *boppli."*

A short time later another cry announced the second little one's arrival followed by shouts of joy and laughter.

Ella and Holly looked at each other and smiled.

"They're here," Holly sniffled, wiping away her tears.

"Jah, I guess they are." Ella paused to wipe away tears of her own. "We are aunts now."

Ella thought about Isaac and her happiness was tinged with sadness. How she wished he were here to witness the miracle of this night.

A half hour passed before Holly and Ella tip toed into Susan's dimly lit bedroom. They paused for a moment just inside the doorway.

Susan lay in bed with the *bopplies* wrapped in blankets and nestled snuggly in her arms. She smiled as they entered the room even though tears slipped down her cheeks. "God has blessed me with a sweet boy and a beautiful girl." Her smile wobbled as she tried to maintain her composure.

Ella moved closer to get a better look at the precious bundles. The babies slept peacefully in Susan's arms. Downy blonde hair covered their heads and faint smiles touched their lips.

Susan bent to kiss each babe in turn. "Isaac and I picked out Grace for a girl's name and Mervin for a boy."

Ella's smile trembled. "Oh, Susan, those are wonderful names."

Susan took a deep breath. "But I have decided to name our little boy, Isaac, after his father."

Mamm choked back a sob. *"Danke,* Susan," she said softly.

"I wish Isaac could be here to witness the birth of our *bopplies,"* Susan sniffled. "He was so looking forward to this day."

Mamm wrapped her arms around her daughter-in-law and they both broke down in tears.

Ella and Holly hugged. In a week's time, they had lost a brother but gained a nephew and a niece.

Ruth bustled around the room gathering up dirty linens and packing up her equipment. She stopped by the bed to gaze at the new arrivals. "They are truly a blessing, *jah?* "

Ella nodded. She bowed her head and silently thanked God for keeping Susan and the babies safe. Once finished, she sat down on the edge of the bed and gave in to her own tears.

Chapter Nine

Ella crawled into bed during the wee hours of the morning. Her eyelids were heavy, but sleep failed to come. Her mind raced with thoughts of Susan and the babies. Would Susan be able to put the pieces of her life back together or would she spend the rest of her days broken and alone?

She sighed heavily as she drifted off to sleep, praying that the Lord would watch out for not only Susan, but the entire family. For in her heart she knew there were dark days ahead. A scripture from Psalms came to her mind and she smiled.

The Lord will keep you from all harm-
he will watch over your life;
the Lord will watch over your coming and going

both now and forevermore.

Holly was sitting at the kitchen table when Ella walked in the next morning. "Are you ready for the quilting frolic?"

Ella gazed at her sister through bleary eyes as she poured herself a cup of *kaffi* and sat down at the table. She yawned before speaking. "What quilting frolic?"

Holly smiled a little too cheerfully for so early in the morning. "The one at Uncle Melvin and Aunt Ada's *haus.*"

Ella shrugged as she looked around the kitchen. "Where's *mamm?*"

"She went over to Susan's the first thing this morning," Holly said, as she finished her breakfast. "She plans to be there the entire day to help with the *bopplies,* but she wants us to attend the frolic and take the batch of peanut butter cookies she baked yesterday."

Ella thought about how much she had missed quilting in the years she had been gone. It used to be one of her favorite past times, but it, like many things over the years, had fallen by the way side during her time spent living in the *Englisch* world.

"Sounds *gut,*" Ella said. "I haven't quilted in years, so I'm not sure how much good I will be, but it should be fun."

"*Jah,* it will be," Holly agreed. "We will be working on quilts for Susan's *bopplies.*" She looked at the way Ella was dressed and frowned. "But you can't wear *that*!"

Ella glanced down at her pink sweater and jeans and shrugged. "I have nothing else to wear and this is conservative enough."

Holly's lips thinned and she shook her head. "*Nee.* People already talk about you enough the way it is, you don't need to add fuel to the fire." She thought for a moment. "Maybe you can wear one of my dresses."

Ella giggled as she pictured herself wearing Holly's dress. Holly towered over her by a good six inches, so any dress of hers would be way too long. "*Danke,* Holly, but I don't think it would fit."

Holly rolled her eyes. "Don't be silly. I know it would be a few inches too long, but we could always pin the hem." She tilted her head to the side and then her eyes sparkled. "Or you could wear the new blue dress I'm making. I've finished everything, but the hem."

Ella looked at her sister. "Can I ask you a question?"

Holly gave her a puzzled look. "Of course."

Ella arched a delicate brow. "Where are all of my old clothes? I know there is still the green dress, but what happened to the rest of my dresses?"

Holly looked embarrassed and stared at the floor. "I burned them," she mumbled.

Ella looked at her sister in shock. "You what? Why on earth would you do such a thing?"

Holly sighed as she met her gaze. "I was angry when you left without saying goodbye." She shrugged. "So one day, I gathered all of your clothes together and burned them in the barrel behind the barn." She looked at Ella apologetically. "But I saved your favorite dress."

Ella didn't know whether to laugh or cry. She began to giggle as she pictured her sister carrying a big bundle of clothes out of the house and burning them in secret.

Holly began to laugh along with her. "I'm sorry. I guess it was kind of a bratty thing to do."

"*Jah,* it was," Ella agreed and gave her sister a hug. "But I can picture myself doing the same thing if the situation had been reversed."

Holly grinned. "I promise to make you new clothes if you stay."

Ella quickly sobered. She hadn't thought much about her future plans. She knew she would be here for the next few months, but by the time fall rolled around, she hoped to have found another teaching job.

Holly frowned and folded her arms across her chest. "You aren't staying, are you?"

Ella sighed, wishing they could return to the light hearted moment of before. "I don't know, Holly. I haven't thought that far ahead."

"What about Noah?" Holly asked as she filled a container with peanut butter cookies in preparation for the quilting frolic.

Ella shrugged. "What about him?"

"Isn't he going to be hurt if you leave again?"

"Noah and I are just friends, Holly."

"But that can change," Holly insisted. "He cares about you, Ella. I know that he does."

"You're forgetting something," Ella said slowly. "Noah is a member of the church. I would have to be baptized in order for us to date, or Noah could be shunned."

"Well," Holly shrugged. "What's wrong with that? You always said if the accident hadn't happened you would have joined the church, so why can't you join it now?"

Ella tried to find the words that would make her sister understand. "I've changed, Holly. I'm not sure if I could fit in to this community anymore. I would like to teach again, if the opportunity arises."

"So you plan to leave us?" Tears filled Holly's eyes. "Once you find a job, you will walk out on your family again."

"*Nee,*" Ella said as tears gathered on her lashes. "I would visit. I promise."

"*Jah,*" Holly said drily. "Just like you visited before."

The ride to Uncle Melvin and Aunt Ada's house was made in silence. Holly rejected Ella's attempts at conversation, so Ella sat, staring out at the barren fields as the buggy slowly rolled by. She was grateful when they finally turned into the drive of their uncle and aunt's cheerful two-story brick home.

Their cousin, Katie, came rushing out to greet them. "I'm so glad you're here." She gave each of them a hug. "What's wrong?" she asked, noticing their frowns.

"Oh, nothing," Holly said as she stomped up on to the porch. "Except that Ella plans to leave as soon as she finds another job."

Katie gasped and looked at Ella with eyes wide. "Is that true?"

"I haven't decided," Ella mumbled, shooting Holly a dark look. Their cousin Katie loved to gossip and the news that she might possibly leave would be all over the community before nightfall.

"But you just got here," Katie pouted as they stepped into the warm kitchen. "I had hoped you planned to stay for good this time."

"Weren't we all," Holly said as she brushed by Ella on her way into the living room.

Ella lingered in the kitchen and watched as Katie prepared chicken salad for the noon meal. From the living room she could hear the mingle of voices as the women of the community worked to make Susan's *bopplies* quilts they would always treasure.

At the mention of her name, Ella moved to the living room doorway. From beyond, she could hear several women of the community discuss her return.

"I can't believe Abram and Gretta Graber let their daughter come home after all the trouble she has caused," a voice Ella recognized as belonging to Elsie Brubaker said. "If she had been my daughter all those years ago, I would have put an end to her wild ways before they even started."

"*Jah,*" one of the other women agreed. "Ella Graber has brought a lot of grief to this community, that's for sure."

Ella's cheeks burned as she backed away from the doorway. She turned and with a muffled sob, yanked open the outside door, stumbling down the porch steps and out into the snow. From behind her Ella could hear Katie calling her name, but she continued on.

Tears leaked from her eyes and froze instantly on her cheeks as she began the long trek home. She briefly thought about turning back and taking the buggy, forcing Holly to find another way home, but decided against it. Why give her sister something else to be mad about.

A buggy approached from the opposite direction. It slowed to a stop and a man jumped down. Ella squinted through the falling snow and saw that it was Noah. He wore a dark frown as he determinedly marched her way.

"Ella." Noah stopped in front of her. "What are you doing out here? Are you trying to freeze to death?"

"*Nee.*" Ella gritted her teeth in an attempt to stop them from chattering. "I'm just taking a little walk."

Noah arched his brows in disbelief as he steered her toward his buggy. "In a snowstorm?"

Ella had to admit the snow was falling faster than before. Large flakes fell swiftly to the ground, so dense she could scarcely see a foot in front of her. "It wasn't snowing this much when I started," she said weakly.

Noah helped her into the buggy and then climbed in beside her. He handed her a blanket to help keep her warm. "Now," he said gently, his blue eyes kind. "Tell me why you are really out here."

Ella sniffled. "There is a quilting frolic at my Uncle Melvin and Aunt Ada's *haus.* I decided to leave early, is all."

"Without your buggy?"

She shrugged. "I left it for Holly."

Noah glanced at her before putting the buggy in motion. "What are you not telling me, Ella?"

"Nothing," Ella said. She felt guilty for lying, but was embarrassed to tell him the truth. Why bring up the past when the memories of that dark day would only cause him pain.

"Ella." Noah's voice was firm. "We're friends, remember? You can talk to me."

Ella's bottom lip trembled. "Some women were talking about the accident that I caused."

"And?" Noah's expression darkened.

"They said that my parents shouldn't have allowed me to return home." Ella paused to wipe away a tear. "They said that I had caused enough pain."

Noah's jaw clenched in anger. "I'm sorry you were treated that way. If you tell me their names, I will have a word with them."

Ella shook her head. "It's my battle, Noah. You can't always solve my problems."

"*Nee,*" Noah said as he glanced her way. "But I would like to, if you would give me the chance."

Ella's breath caught in her throat. "What are you saying?"

Noah sighed. "I can't stop thinking about the way things were between us and while I know we can only be friends as long as you are not a member of the church. I would still like to spend time with you." He hesitated. "That is, if it's alright with you?"

Ella smiled softly. *"Jah,* I would like that."

"Gut." Noah nodded as if the matter was settled.

Ella couldn't stop smiling as the buggy traveled slowly toward home. Maybe she and Noah could mend their tattered relationship.

She closed her eyes and began to pray.

Chapter Ten

Noah became a fixture in Ella's life.

The next few weeks passed in a whirlwind of buggy rides and long talks. Ella felt blessed to have his company and looked forward to the time they spent together even if they were only friends.

Noah had forgiven her. Whatever dark thoughts may have remained from that rainy night long ago, he had faced them and found peace. Ella only wished she could do the same.

The tantalizing smell of freshly brewed coffee roused her from a sound sleep. Sitting up, she yawned and squinted her eyes at the alarm clock.

Five o'clock.

Grumbling, Ella sat on the edge of the bed and willed away the last traces of sleep. She had never been a morning person but days began early around the farm and it was beginning to take a toll.

With a sigh, she dressed and padded downstairs to find that *Mamm,* Holly, Faith and Corrine already had breakfast preparations well under way.

"Sorry, I'm late," Ella murmured.

Their father was putting on his coat and boots before he went out to tend to the horses. *"Guder mariye,"* he said, his eyes twinkling.

"Good morning, *Daed."* Ella gave him a hug. "How are you on this fine morning?"

He smiled. "I don't have any complaints. I am blessed with a wonderful wife, beautiful daughters and healthy grandchildren. A man can't ask for more."

Ella turned to her mother. "Would you mind if I helped *daed* with the chores?"

"Ach, *nee.*" *Mamm* waved the spatula she was using to flip over the eggs. "Go with your father. We can handle things here."

Ella followed her father out of the house and down the narrow shoveled path to the barn. Once there, she walked over to Midnight's empty stall and leaned on the stall door.

How many times had Midnight greeted her in the morning with a friendly nicker and loyal gaze? She had betrayed his trust, just like she had betrayed the trust of her family and friends.

Her father finished feeding and watering the horses and came to stand beside her. "You miss your horse, *jah*?"

"Jah, I do." Ella wiped a tear from her cheek.

Her father nodded. "Well, maybe if you decide to stay we can buy you another horse."

They hadn't spoken about her future plans during the weeks she had been home. Her car was parked behind the barn and hadn't been driven since the day of her arrival, but she wasn't certain what choice she should make. Should she stay here amongst her family and community or should she leave and have the opportunity to once again use the degree she had worked so hard to obtain? It was a decision she wasn't sure she was ready to make.

A lump formed in her throat. "I'm torn, *daed.* I love living here again, but a part of me isn't ready to commit to the Amish way of life."

"Nonsense." Her father waved away her concerns with a flick of his hand. "What is there to be uncertain about? You were raised here, Ella. This is where you belong."

Ella walked over to watch the softly falling snow through the barn's open door. "But I also want to be able to use my teaching degree."

Her father scratched his beard. "That is a problem, to be certain. You won't be able to use your teaching degree in the community without first committing to the church."

Ella glanced back at her father and noticed for the first time the tired lines around his eyes. He had worked hard through the years to provide for his family and she couldn't shake the feeling she was letting him down.

She hesitated. "I want to stay, really I do, but I'm not ready to join the church."

Her father nodded. "It is an important decision you have to make and one you shouldn't make on your own. Have you prayed on this matter, daughter?"

Ella met his solemn gaze. "I have, but I'm still just as confused as ever."

Her father gave a slight smile. "Well, I'm sure the Lord will answer you in His own time." He patted her on the shoulder. "About time to go inside for breakfast, don't you think?"

The walk from the barn to the house was a silent one. Even though her father didn't say another word about the subject, Ella knew he would support her decision no matter what the outcome.

Ella smiled as they stepped into the kitchen and were wrapped in the comforting warmth from the wood stove and surrounded by the delicious smells of the food that had been prepared. She loved mornings when the family was all together before they tackled the trials of the day.

Mamm set a platter of fried eggs, sausage, and bacon on the table as they sat down. A basket of buttery biscuits soon followed.

Daed signaled the silent blessing and they all lowered their heads. After a few minutes, he cleared his throat and they began to fill their plates.

"Corrine," their mother said around a mouthful of eggs. "Don't dawdle, or you will be late for *schul.*"

Corrine frowned. "Do I have to go to school today? I want to go see Susan and the *bopplies.*"

"Hush, now," *Mamm* gently scolded her youngest daughter. "There will be plenty of time to see your new niece and nephew after school."

A buggy pulled up outside.

Faith jumped up and went to the window. "Ethan Miller is here and Noah just pulled up beside him."

Their father wiped his mouth with a napkin and pushed away from the table. "Your grandfather and I hired Ethan to work in the shop. Today is his first day."

Mamm made a sound of distress.

"It's time, Gretta," he said gently.

Ella walked to the window and peeked out. She remembered Ethan Miller being a rather rambunctious, short twelve year old boy the last time she had seen him. Today, he was well over six feet tall and all signs of hyper activity appeared to have vanished.

"Wasn't Ethan in your grade in school?" Holly teased Faith.

Faith shrugged and walked away from the window. *"Jah.* So?"

Holly glanced out the window at the young man. "He's pretty cute."

"Faith only has eyes for Gideon Wyse." Corrine giggled.

"I do not!" Faith snapped.

"Girls." Their mother frowned. "That will be enough of this kind of talk."

Ella studied her younger sister. She hadn't had a clue Faith was interested in Noah's younger brother and was surprised to find it didn't sit well with her. As the youngest, Gideon Wyse had always been a bit spoiled and she felt in her heart that nothing good could come from their relationship.

Mamm jumped up from the table. "Corrine, you need to hurry or you will be late for school."

She placed a kiss on her youngest daughter's cheek. "Holly and Faith, please take the cookies and pies we baked yesterday to the bake sale and explain to the women that I'm helping Susan with the *bopplies*."

She turned to Ella. "I'm going over to Susan's for the day. Your grandmother's arthritis is bothering her and I need you to stay here and help her clean. You can fix sandwiches for the *menner* for lunch. There is ham and roast beef in the refrigerator and they can have some of the cookies we baked for dessert."

"*Jah, mamm.*" Ella took another peek out the window hoping to see Noah, but found the yard empty.

Chapter Eleven

Ella didn't have much time to think about Noah as she spent the morning helping her grandmother wash the walls in the *grossdaadi haus.* Truth be told, she was the only one completing the chore, while her grandmother sat in her favorite chair and gave directions, but Ella didn't mind. Her grandmother had spent many years doing household chores and had earned a little rest.

At ten o'clock, her grandmother motioned for her to stop work, and poured a couple cups of coffee. Next she put out a plate of snickerdoodle cookies. "About time for a break, ain't so?"

Ella sank wearily into a chair. "*Jah.* A break would be welcome."

"You must be getting soft, child," her grandmother chided. "You use to be able to work all morning without getting tired."

Ella met her grandmother's amused gaze. "Maybe I'm just getting old."

"Could be." Her grandmother winked.

Grandmother Graber took a bite out of a cookie and peered at Ella over the top of her glasses. "It's good to have you home, Ella. You were away for far too long."

Ella took a sip of coffee. "I'm happy to be home too. There are a lot of nice things about the *Englisch* world, but nothing can replace the ones you love."

Grandmother nodded. "I agree. I see you've grown wise in the years you've been gone."

Ella smiled. "Well, I don't know about that, but I did learn a few things about what is important to me and what isn't." She nibbled on a snickerdoodle. "I told *daed* I loved living here and I'm not sure I want to leave."

"*Das gut.*" Her grandmother smiled. "Your father has waited a long time to hear those words. He never stopped praying for you to return home."

Ella lowered head. "I'm sorry for all the pain I've caused the family. I hadn't planned to be gone for so long."

Grandmother patted her arm. "None of us are perfect. We've all caused pain to another person at one time or another."

Ella looked out the window at the snowflakes falling steadily past. "I can't believe how much snow we've gotten this winter."

Grandmother laughed. "You young folk aren't accustomed to lots of snow. When I was a girl, winters were cold and harsh with a lot of precipitation. Snow fell around Thanksgiving and didn't melt until spring."

"I bet you had fun as a child." She tried to picture her grandmother as a little girl playing in the snow, but couldn't.

"Grandmother's eyes twinkled. "I remember one winter we had so much snow it covered the downstairs windows. My father had to tunnel a path to the barn so he could feed the animals. My sisters, brothers and I, spent several days creating a tunnel of snow from one bedroom window to another." She laughed. "Boy, were we in trouble when our mother finally caught us."

Ella giggled. "I don't think we've ever had that much snow."

Her grandmother chuckled. "Just don't tell your *daed*. I seem to recall scolding him and your

Uncle Melvin for doing the same thing one winter."

Ella smiled and shook her head. "I won't. I promise."

Grandmother held a hand to her ear. "Is that the men folk I hear?"

Ella jumped up and raced to the door connecting the *grossdaadi haus* to the main house. "Oh, my goodness. I completely lost track of time. The men are coming inside for lunch and I don't have a thing ready."

Grandmother waved away her concern. "Calm down, child. It doesn't take long to make sandwiches. I will come over and help you."

The men were sitting at the table nursing cups of coffee when Ella and her grandmother walked into the kitchen. They laughed and joked as they talked amongst themselves.

Ella bustled around the kitchen as she fixed a platter piled high with sliced ham, roast beef and cheese. She also put out bread that had been baked the day before and a bowl of pasta salad. There was coffee and sweet tea to drink. The last thing on the table was a plate of chocolate chunk cookies.

After the blessing, Ella asked Ethan how he liked working in the shop.

"I like it just fine." He gave her a warm smile that lit up his brown eyes. "I've always liked making things."

Ella returned his smile and wondered why Faith couldn't be interested in a young man such as this. "Weren't you and Faith in the same grade in *schul*?" she asked, even though she already knew the answer.

"Jah. We were." Ethan's face brightened. He looked around. "So, uh…is Faith here?"

"Nee." Ella shook her head. "She and Holly went to a bake sale that is being held to help raise funds for our sister-in-law, Susan."

Ethan's face fell. "Well, please tell her I said hello."

Ella smiled, cheered by the interest he had shown in her sister. "I will be sure and do that." She looked across the table at Noah who was regarding her with a frown. She gave him a big smile, but only received a darker frown in return.

Ella shrugged and resumed eating.

Before long the meal was over and the men headed back outside to work.

Noah paused by the porch door. "Ella? May I ask you something?" He tipped his chin in her direction.

Grandmother Graber got up from the table. "I think I will go back to the *grossdaadi haus* and give you young folk some privacy," she said with a smile, before leaving through the connecting door.

Ella walked over to join him. "*Jah.* You can."

Noah cleared his throat and glanced around before meeting her gaze. "Are you interested in Ethan Miller?"

"What? Noah, you can't be serious. I'm six years older than him."

He gave a lop-sided grin. "Well, I'm older than you."

Ella waved away the information. "Oh, that's different and you know it. Besides, there are only four years between us, not six."

He breathed a sigh of relief and nodded. "That's true, but I had to ask."

She tilted her head. "Is that all you wanted to ask me?"

Noah paused for a moment. "Would you like to go to a sledding party at Wayne and Miriam Bontrager's? It might be the last this season."

Ella smiled. "As friends?"

He looked a little sheepish. "I know we have no business being anything other than friends. I am a member of the church and you are not, but I can't deny how I feel about you. How I still feel about you, even after all this time."

Her breath caught. "Are you sure?"

Noah regarded her soberly. *"Jah.* I am."

Ella wanted to do a little dance, but instead managed to say, "I would love to, but aren't we a little old?"

Noah shook his head and grinned, tilting his head to one side. *"Nee.* We are not too old.

There will be plenty of people at the party who are our age and older."

Ella returned his smile. "Well, if that is the case, *jah,* of course I will go with you. I haven't been sledding in a long time."

"Great. I will pick you up tomorrow." He leaned over and kissed her cheek before heading out the door.

"Thank you, God," she whispered.

Chapter Twelve

It had been a long cold winter. Ella sighed as she looked at the mounds of snow piled along the sidewalk leading to Bishop Burkholder's front door.

She twisted her hands nervously as she stood on the Bishop's front porch. Was she making the right choice? And would the leader of their community agree with her decision to join the church or would he chastise her for not attending as often as she should?

"Ella." The front door opened to reveal Iris Burkholder. "What a wonderful surprise on this fine morning. Please, come in out of the cold."

"*Danke,* Iris." Ella was grateful to step into the Burkholder's warm kitchen.

"How are your parents?" Iris poured a couple of cups of coffee and placed a plate of sliced banana bread on the table. She motioned for her to take a seat.

"*Mamm* says she is fine, but I still hear her crying in the middle of the night."

Iris gave her a sympathetic look. "Well, that is to be expected. It isn't easy losing a child."

Ella remembered that Iris and the Bishop had lost their only child, David, in a farming accident a few years ago. David had been a couple of years behind her in school, and had always been kind hearted.

"I'm sorry. I had forgotten you had suffered a loss as well."

Iris patted the tears away from her eyes. "A parent never gets over losing a child, that is for sure, but the Lord helps us endure." She smiled.

"I will have to stop by and visit your mother. Maybe it will help if she talks to a mother who understands what she is going through."

"*Danke.* I'm sure *mamm* will welcome your visit."

Iris took a sip of coffee. "So, what has brought you by on such a cold and dreary morning?"

Ella hesitated. "Well, I had hoped to speak with the Bishop if he is available."

Iris smiled. "Of course, child. He will be happy to speak with you. He had planned to stop by your house in a few days, but I'm sure he will speak with you now." She rose from the table and left the room, only to come back a few minutes later with the bishop in tow.

"Ella." Bishop Burkholder smiled. "What can I do for you?" He sat down at the table and accepted a cup of *kaffi* from his wife.

Iris excused herself and went into the other room to give them some privacy.

Suddenly nervous, Ella stared at her hands.

"Ella." The Bishop's tone was gentle. "I've known you since you were a little girl. Surely there is no reason for you to be anxious around me?"

"*Nee.*" She met his kind gaze. "I wish to speak to you about joining the church."

The Bishop gave her a serious look. "*Vell,* it might be a *gut* idea for you to begin attending church regularly. I don't believe I've seen you attend service since you've been back home."

Ella flushed. "*Nee.* I haven't gone, but that is going to change."

"I should hope so." He paused as he took a drink of coffee. "Especially since you are seeing Noah Wyse again."

She gasped in surprise. "You know I've been seeing Noah?"

He chuckled. "News travels fast in this community. Maybe I should preach a sermon on the trouble idle gossip can cause." He quickly sobered. "Are you aware that Noah is a minister in the church?"

Ella was shocked. "*Nee,* he hasn't mentioned it."

The Bishop leaned back in his chair. "Now, that is troubling. I would have thought Noah would have told you by now. You are aware that he is violating church rules by courting you?"

She nodded.

"His mother is concerned about your relationship. She is afraid that you will have a negative influence on her young grandson."

Ella flinched. She was well aware of Martha Wyse's ill feelings toward her, but she couldn't believe Martha thought her grandson would be harmed by associating with her.

"I'm sorry she feels that way." Her voice was a mere whisper.

"Well, I plan to stop by and speak to her about the matter, but I'm not certain it will do much good. You caused a great deal of hurt in her life and I'm not convinced she will ever find it in her heart to forgive."

Ella turned her head as tears filled her eyes.

The Bishop reached across the table and patted her hand. "Now, what is it I hear about you having a teaching degree?"

She gave a wobbly smile. "I have a bachelor degree in elementary education from Purdue University."

He smiled. "You always were a smart one. I bet you are anxious to put that degree to use now that you are back in the community?"

She nodded. "I would love to teach again, but there aren't that many teaching jobs around here."

"Well, now." The Bishop leaned back in his chair and stroked his beard. "There might be an opening at the school next fall."

Her hopes soared.

"Our current teacher, Annie Lambright, plans on leaving at the end of this term and the school board will need to fill her position."

Ella fairly bounced in her chair. "Do you think if I apply there will be a chance I will be offered the position?"

The Bishop smiled. "Well, first things first. Right now you need to concentrate on attending church and becoming a member. I will expect you to go through the baptismal classes this spring."

"*Jah,* of course. I've thought it over and I am ready to become a baptized member of this community."

He nodded. "I'm happy to hear that, child. As for the teaching position, I can't give you an answer until you are a church member. Once you are a member, you are welcome to submit an application to the school board for review."

She smiled. "*Danke.*" Pushing back her chair she rose and prepared to leave. "Please tell Iris thank you for the coffee and banana bread and I will be sure to tell my mother to expect her visit."

The Bishop nodded and followed her to the door. "I will be sure to do that. Please tell your parents to stop by anytime if they need to talk."

Ella nodded and stepped out into the winter air. She climbed into her buggy and meditated on a scripture as she steered the buggy home.

Ask, and it will be given to you; seek and you will find; knock, and it will be opened to you.

Chapter Thirteen

The day of the sledding party dawned bright and cold. Ella awoke with a headache and groaned as she threw back the covers. She slowly dressed and went downstairs to help her mother and sisters with breakfast.

Holly looked up from setting the table as Ella walked into the kitchen. "You look awful."

Ella grimaced, holding a hand to her head. "Gee. Thanks for the compliment."

Mamm turned around from the stove. "Holly is right, you do look awful." She put down her spatula and walked over to feel Ella's forehead. "Ach, you have a fever."

Ella sank down onto the nearest chair. "*Nee.* I can't be sick," she moaned. "Today is the sledding party."

"I don't think you are in any condition to attend a sledding party." Her mother walked over to a cupboard and took down a bottle of aspirin. She took two out and then got a glass of water. She walked back over and handed them to Ella.

"*Danke, mamm,*" Ella murmured, still holding her head.

Her mother folded her arms. "Did you take you other medication?"

Ella sighed. "*Jah.* I did." It had been years since her mother had asked her if she had taken the medicine to treat her bipolar disorder and she had to admit, she had missed the gentle reminders."

"*Gut.*" *Mamm* grasped her arm and steered her toward the doorway. "Now the only place you need to be is in bed."

Ella reluctantly climbed the stairs and crawled back in bed. Feverishly, she prayed that she would be better by evening so she would be able to attend the sledding party. She slept fitfully throughout the day. Dreams about Noah and the accident swirled in her head creating a dark nightmare she could not escape.

Evening shadows bathed the room the next time she opened her eyes. Holly was brushing her hair and turned when she made a sound.

"I wish you felt well enough to come to the party with us." Holly crossed the room to sit on the edge of her bed. "Uncle Melvin dropped Katie off so she could go with us to the party and then spend the night afterwards."

Ella could hear Katie's voice as it floated up from downstairs. She struggled to sit up, but sank back when her head began to swim. "I wish I could go too, but I don't feel any better than I did this morning." She knew Noah would be disappointed, but she was in no condition to attend a party.

Holly finished fixing her hair. "I plan on taking our buggy, but Faith will probably go with Gideon and Noah when they arrive." She walked over to give Ella a hug. "I will tell you all about it when I get back."

"Danke, Holly," Ella mumbled as she ducked back beneath the covers and promptly fell asleep.

Hours drifted past before she once again opened her eyes. Dark shadows encased the room and the house lay silent around her. She looked towards Holly's bed and saw that it was empty.

Throwing back the covers, Ella slipped out of bed and shivered as her bare feet came in contact with the cold floor boards. Crossing the room, she looked out the window just in time to see Holly walking from the barn to the house. She slipped back into bed a minute before Holly entered the room. "So, how was the party?"

Holly jumped. "I thought you were asleep!" She quickly changed her clothes and slid into her bed. "The party was a lot of fun. I wish you could have been there."

"Where are Faith and Katie?"

"They wanted to stay a little longer, so Gideon promised to bring them home. He and Noah brought separate buggies."

Ella eyed her sister as best as she could in the dim lighting. She could tell Holly wasn't telling her something.

"What about Noah? Did he stay at the party?"

Holly yawned loudly. "Can we talk about this in the morning? I'm really tired and I just want to go to sleep."

Ella picked up her pillow and threw it at her sister. "*Nee*. We can't talk about it in the morning. Now, what about Noah?"

"He said he is sorry you are sick." Holly said, avoiding the question.

"And?"

"That was all he said."

Frustrated, Ella stalked across the room to retrieve her pillow. "That was it? He didn't say anything else to you?"

"Ella, there is something you should know."
Holly's words hung in the air between them.
"Noah didn't leave the sledding party alone."

Ella turned to her in disbelief. "What do you
mean?"

"He left with Megan Zehr."

Ella sat down on her bed and struggled to
make sense of it all. "Maybe Megan needed a
ride home and Noah was just being nice?"

"*Nee.*" Holly sighed. "Katie and I both
overheard him ask Megan if he could give her a
ride home." She was silent for a moment.
"Megan said she had a way home, but Noah
insisted."

"Why would he do that?" Ella hopped back
out of bed and began to pace. "Why would he
ask to spend time with me if he still wishes to
court Megan?"

Holly groaned and buried her head underneath the covers. "Can we *please* talk about this in the morning?"

Tears welled in Ella's eyes. Maybe Noah didn't care for her the way she did for him. She pulled the covers up around her head and closed her eyes.

"I'm sorry, Ella." Holly whispered, but got no response.

Chapter Fourteen

Ella was silent the next morning during breakfast, much preferring to sit and listen to Faith and Katie talk about the party and all the fun they had sledding down the hill behind the Bontrager's house. After a great deal of thinking and praying, she had decided not to let the fact that Noah had taken Megan home bring her down.

"We had such fun," Katie gushed. "Wayne Bontrager lit a fire and we roasted hot dogs and marshmallows and sipped hot chocolate."

"I wish I could have gone." Corrine pouted.

"There will be plenty of sledding parties in your future." *Mamm* kissed her daughter's cheek. "How would you like to miss school today and visit Susan and the *bopplies?*"

"Can I?" Corrine's eyes glowed with excitement.

"I don't see why not. I'm sure it won't hurt if you miss one day. Now finish up your breakfast so we can get going." She turned to address her niece. "Katie, we will drop you off at your home on the way to Susan's. I'm sure your mother has a list of chores for you to do today."

"*Danke,* Aunt Gretta," Katie murmured.

Daed put down his coffee cup and looked at Ella. "A neighbor stopped by yesterday while you were sick and wanted to know if you planned to sell your car."

Ella chewed her lower lip. Her car was her last link with the *Englisch* world. Selling it would help prove to the Bishop and the community that she planned to stay.

"*Jah.* I do plan to sell it."

"Gut." Her father looked pleased. "He said he would stop by the shop this afternoon to find out your decision." He rose from the table and prepared to leave for work.

"I can't believe you are selling your car," Holly said after their father had left the house. "I guess this means you're serious about staying, huh?"

"Jah." Ella smiled. "I guess I am." She took her breakfast dishes over to the sink to be washed. "I talked to Bishop Burkholder about taking baptismal classes this spring."

"Ella, that's wonderful!" Holly gave her a quick hug. *"Mamm* and *Daed* will be so happy."

Their mother walked back into the room and quickly packed a basket filled with sweet rolls and various kinds of cookies to take to Susan's. Lastly, she picked up a cake pan holding a chocolate cake she had baked the night before.

"You girls can finish the breakfast dishes then please start on the laundry," she said as she was going out the door.

Ella waited until her mother's buggy was a good distance down the road, then grabbed her coat.

"Where are you going?" Holly asked, wiping her hands on the dish towel.

"To speak to Noah."

"*Daed* isn't going to like it if you bother them while they are working."

"I'll just be a minute." Ella slipped outside into the bright sunshine.

Noah wasn't around when she walked in the front door of Graber's Furniture. The showroom was spotless, but she could hear the sounds of hammering and male laughter coming from the back.

"Can I help you, Ella?" Ethan Miller emerged from the back room and gave her a boyish grin.

"*Danke,* Ethan, but, *nee.*" She returned his smile. "I need to speak with Noah."

"Uh, sure. I guess it would be okay. Just go on back."

Ella stepped into the back room, noting her father and grandfather's looks of surprise.

"Is something wrong, Ella?" her father asked with concern.

"*Nee, daed.* Everything is fine. I just need to speak to Noah for a minute, that's all."

Her father shook his head, but motioned for her to step further into the room. "We are behind on orders, so please don't talk long."

"This will hardly take any time at all. I promise." Ella walked over to where Noah was sanding on a beautiful oak headboard. His dark head bent over the piece as he concentrated on his task. She watched him work for a minute, fascinated by the way his hands expertly glided over the furniture before giving a discreet cough.

"Is there something you need, Ella?" he asked without looking up.

"Can I speak with you for a minute?"

He raised his head and their gazes locked. "Go ahead."

"Outside?"

"I'm really busy. Like you *daed* said, we are behind on orders."

Ella wasn't backing down. "Please?"

Noah sighed, but nodded and followed her outside.

Cold air whipped around them as she turned to face him, arms folded. "So, how was the sledding party?"

His forehead wrinkled. "You came over here to ask me about the party?"

"*Jah.* So, how was it?"

"It was okay," Noah said, wiping his hands clean with a rag. "It would have been better if you had been there with me."

"See anyone special?"

Noah ran a hand along his bearded jaw. "Does this have anything to do with the fact that I took Megan home last night?"

Ella tapped her foot in frustration. The man had no right to look so handsome with the sun glinting off his dark hair when she was so mad at him. "*Jah,* it does. Holly said that Megan already had a way home, but you insisted on taking her."

"*Jah.* I did. Her house is on my way home, so it wasn't a bother."

Ella felt some of the wind go out of her sails. She was acting like a child, not a twenty-four year old woman, who just a few weeks ago was teaching in an elementary school classroom.

"Noah, I'm sorry. I just thought...well, I don't know what I thought. I just know that I didn't like the idea of you spending time with Megan."

A corner of Noah's mouth quirked upward in a grin. Humor crinkled his eyes. His tone softened. "Jealous, much?"

"*Jah.*" She shrugged. "I guess I am."

He gently pulled her to him and enfolded her in his arms. Tilting up her chin, he brushed his lips gently across hers before placing a kiss on her temple. He raised his head, his warm breath fanning her face. "There will never be a reason for you to be jealous, Ella. You are the only one for me."

A loud cough came from behind them. They both turned to find her father regarding them with a slight frown.

He addressed Noah first. "Best be getting back to work, don't you think?"

Noah nodded and began to open the shop door, then stopped. "May I stop by your house tonight?"

Ella's heart skipped a beat. *"Jah,* of course you can. You are welcome to stay for dinner if you like."

He smiled. *"Danke.* I would like that. Hopefully by then I will have some good news to tell you." With that, he disappeared back inside.

With an embarrassed look, Ella faced her father. "I'm sorry for taking Noah away from his work, *Daed."*

Her father's frown deepened. "It isn't taking Noah away from his work that I am concerned about."

Her heart sank.

"It isn't proper for you and Noah to carry on in such a manner. Noah is a member of the church, but even if he were not, he shouldn't be kissing you."

"It won't happen again, *daed.*"

Her father nodded. "See that it doesn't." He opened the door and went inside.

Ella couldn't keep the smile off of her face as she walked backed to the house. Noah had practically said he loved her. She was so close to getting everything she had ever wanted in life. So why was she afraid she could suddenly lose it all?

Chapter Fifteen

Ella bustled around the kitchen putting the finishing touches on a dinner of fried chicken, biscuits, mashed potatoes with gravy and peach pie. She could scarcely believe how different her life was from a couple of months ago. Before, she would have come home to an empty apartment, heated a frozen dinner and eaten it alone in front of the television. Now, she was surrounded by family and a wonderful man who cared for her.

Faith twirled into the kitchen. "A buggy just pulled up." She peered out the kitchen window.

"Noah is coming to dinner."

Faith made a face. "I thought Noah was still seeing Megan Zehr?"

"*Nee.* He isn't."

Faith shook her head. "I don't know, Ella. Gideon seems to think Noah is still courting Megan. He said their mother still hasn't forgiven you for the accident and doesn't want to have you as a daughter-in-law."

Ella felt like she had been slapped. Oblivious to the company outside, she sat down on the nearest chair and tried to make sense of her sister's words. She blinked back tears. "When did Gideon tell you this?"

"When he brought me home from the sledding party." Faith walked over and gave her a hug. "I'm sorry. I didn't mean to make you cry."

Ella got to her feet. "I'm fine. I know Martha Wyse still blames me for her son and husband's deaths, but maybe over time she will begin to forgive."

Faith looked as if she might cry. "I don't think so, Ella. I know Martha is one of our mother's best friends, but I don't feel she won't ever welcome you as a daughter-in-law."

There was a sharp knock on the door.

Ella pasted on a smile and walked over to greet their guest. "Welcome, Noah," she said as she opened the door.

Noah smiled at the woman in front of him. She never failed to steal his breath and if he had his way, she would hold an important place in his heart for a long time to come. "Thank you for inviting me." He stepped into the kitchen's warm interior.

Gretta Graber breezed into the kitchen. "I'm so happy you could join us for dinner tonight, Noah. How is your *mamm*?"

"She is *gut*. *Danke* for asking. *Mamm* wanted me to remind you about the work frolic she is having at our house next Monday."

"I haven't forgotten." Gretta smiled. "Please tell your *mamm* I plan on bringing marble cake and oatmeal cookies, but if she needs me to bring anything else, just let me know."

Noah smiled at the woman who looked like an older version of Ella. "I'll be certain to tell her."

Abram walked into the kitchen and clapped a hand on Noah's shoulder. "I hope your errand this afternoon had a satisfactory outcome?" He motioned for Noah to take a seat at the table.

"*Jah,* it did." Noah flashed a broad smile. "I'm now the owner of the old Fisher property."

"Noah, that's wonderful. You and Luke are going to love living there." Ella took a seat across from him at the table.

"You're going to want more hours at the shop from now on, I expect." Grandfather Graber shook Noah's hand.

"*Jah*," Noah agreed. "I will be thankful for any hours you can give me, that's for sure."

They lowered their heads for the silent blessing. After a few minutes, Abram coughed to signal prayer time was over and they began to fill their plates.

"Church will be held at Jonas and Anna Beiler's this Sunday." *Mamm* addressed her daughters. "We will go over tomorrow morning and help Anna get the house ready for company."

The girls all nodded except for Corrine who wore a dark frown.

"I wanted you to take me to the library tomorrow," Corrine whined to her mother.

"That will have to wait for another day," *Mamm* said briskly. "After we help at the Beiler's in the morning, we need to stop by Susan's and see if she needs any assistance with the *bopplies*."

Corrine's face brightened. "*Jah,* that sounds like fun."

"It will be *gut* to see Susan and the *bopplies*," Ella agreed. "I bet the babies have grown a ton since we saw them last."

"*Jah*." Their mother nodded. "Babies grow quickly, that's for sure. It doesn't seem that long ago that Corrine was a baby."

Corrine wrinkled her nose. "I'm ten. I haven't been a baby for a long time."

Their *daed* smiled. "*Nee*, you haven't. You've all grown up too fast."

They finished dinner and after a dessert of cheesecake brownies, the women began to clear the table.

Noah cleared his throat. "Ella? Would you like to go on a short ride with me? I was thinking we could go check out my new property."

Ella smiled. *"Jah,* Noah. I would like that, but I have to finish the dishes first."

Mamm waved her hand. "Go see the property. Your sisters and I can finish up here."

A short time later, Noah grinned as they pulled into the driveway of the old farmhouse. "I can't believe it's mine." He helped Ella down from the buggy. "I've always wanted my own place, but I can't believe the day is finally here."

"I'm happy for you." Ella slipped her hand into Noah's as they walked up the sidewalk to the front door. She was thrilled when he didn't pull his hand away.

Noah unlocked the heavy door and ushered her inside. "Well, this is it." He waited anxiously for her response.

Ella peered at the spacious kitchen. Faded paint peeled from the walls and there appeared to be mouse droppings on the counter, but she could picture what this room would look like with a table filled with *kenner*.

"It's wonderful." She walked through the doorway into the next room. It was a large family room with two south facing windows. A wood stove sat in the far corner.

Noah grinned. "It will take a lot of work to fix, but I figure if I work evenings and weekends I should have the place livable by spring. Both your father and grandfather have offered to help and I'm sure I can talk Gideon into working some evenings."

"This will be a *gut* place for you and Luke to have a home." Ella ran a hand over the wooden banister leading to the second floor.

Noah's expression became serious. He walked over to take her hand. "I don't want this to be just mine and Luke's home, Ella. I want this to be your home as well."

Her breath caught. "What are you saying?"

Noah swallowed and for the first time since she had known him, he appeared nervous. "I know this place doesn't look like much right now, but I will fix it. I promise. What I'm trying to say is...Ella, will you marry me?"

"*Jah!*" She threw her arms around him. "I will."

He let out a whoop as he picked her up and twirled her around. Placing a kiss on her lips, he gazed into her eyes and smiled. "You don't know how long I have waited to hear those words."

Ella quickly sobered and took a step back. "Noah? You understand that my doctor might advise me not to have children, because of the medicine I take to treat my bipolar disorder? Some of the medications might be harmful to a developing baby."

Noah was silent for a moment, then he gave her a soft grin. "Ella. I want to marry you, because I love you. Whether or not you can have children doesn't change my feelings for you."

"You love me?" It seemed as if she had waited a lifetime to hear those words.

"I never stopped loving you." Noah's voice was husky with emotion.

"Are you sure?" Ella wiped away the tears that were clinging to her lashes. "I don't want you to resent me later, because I can't give you a son or daughter."

He pulled her back into his arms and gave her a sound kiss. *"Jah.* I've never been more certain of anything in my life."

Ella kissed him back. "I guess I made the right decision in speaking to Bishop Burkholder about taking baptismal classes this spring."

Noah's face clouded. "I want you to join the church, because you want to, not because of me."

She touched his forehead, smoothing away the frown lines. "I've already spoken to the bishop about taking the classes. I've decided that this is where I've always belonged. Here. In this community."

Noah placed another kiss on her lips, then smiled. "This will be a wonderful place to for us to live, *jah?*"

"*Jah*," Ella whispered. "It will be."

Chapter Sixteen

The distinct smell of cigarette smoke greeted Noah when he stepped into the barn the next morning. He sighed as he followed the bluish smoke over to the ladder leading to the haymow. With a silent groan, he began to climb.

Gideon stubbed out the cigarette with the toe of his shoe when he saw Noah's head clear the top of the ladder.

"Watcha got there, little brother?" Noah walked over to stand in front of Gideon.

"Nothing." Gideon shoved the pack of cigarettes deep into his pocket.

Noah frowned. "Come on, Gideon. I'm not stupid. I know you were smoking."

Gideon folded his arms and glared at his older brother. "I guess you caught me."

Noah's frown deepened. "Hand them over."

Gideon lifted his chin a notch. "*Nee.* I'm eighteen. I can smoke if I want."

Noah sighed. Over the past six years he had often acted like a surrogate father to Gideon, but recently his brother had become a little hard to handle.

"You know *mamm* doesn't want you smoking and since this is her property, you need to respect her wishes."

Gideon snorted. "*Jah,* well, maybe I'll leave. I'm getting tired of being treated like I'm still a baby."

A cold chill snaked up Noah's spine. This wasn't the first time Gideon had talked about leaving. "You're willing to hurt *mamm?*" He looked his little brother in the eye. "You know your leaving would devastate her."

Gideon shuffled his feet then shrugged. "I don't want to hurt *mamm*, but she will have you and Audry."

"What about Faith?" Noah knew he was grasping at straws, but he had to try.

A smile crossed Gideon's face. "I do like Faith, but who's to say she won't decide to come with me?"

Noah rubbed the back of his neck and sighed. "Gideon. You can't be serious? What would the two of you possibly do out in the world?"

Gideon smirked. "I'm not as helpless as you think, *bruder.* I'm sure I can find a job working construction."

"How do you think Abram and Gretta Graber will feel?" Noah ran a hand through his hair in frustration. "They've just lost their son, they don't need to lose a daughter as well."

Gideon gave another shrug.

"I'm going to ask Ella to speak to you. She can tell you how hard it is in the *Englisch* world without the help of family or community."

Gideon's face hardened. *"Nee.* I don't want to speak to Ella," he spat the words. "I don't *ever* want to speak to Ella."

Noah's brows rose in surprise. "I thought you liked Ella?"

Gideon shook his head as he walked over to sit on a hay bale. *"Nee.* I don't. At least not anymore."

"I don't know what to say." Noah's eyes pleaded with his brother. "I love Ella and I've asked her to marry me."

Gideon gave his brother a look of disgust. "I don't like her, Noah. *Mamm* doesn't like her. I can't believe you want to marry that woman after she has taken so much from this family."

"You can't blame Ella for something that was God's will."

Gideon snorted. "That's nonsense and you know it. The only one to blame for the accident is Ella Graber and now you want to bring her into the family."

"What does Faith think about your ill feelings toward her sister? She can't be too happy."

"I haven't told her."

Noah gazed at his brother with concern. "Don't you think you should?"

"Why?" Gideon challenged. "We both plan on leaving, so it won't matter."

For the first time Noah began to worry that his little brother just might follow through with his threat. When had Gideon slipped away from their family and their values? It had happened so slowly, that no one had even noticed.

Gideon shook his head. "You don't know what it's like, Noah. You were already grown when *daed* and Caleb died." He blinked back tears. "Sometimes I lie awake at night and try to picture *daed's* face, but I can't. Caleb's is a little easier because he looked so much like you."

Noah placed a hand on his brother's shoulder. "I'm sorry the past few years have been so hard on you. I guess I spent the first couple of years too lost in my own grief to pay much attention to the people around me."

Gideon angrily swiped at his tears. "*Mamm* has changed so much since the accident. She doesn't laugh anymore."

Noah had noticed the changes in their mother's demeanor. Her sadness hadn't dissipated over the years, if anything, it had grown. "She has changed, *jah*, but we all have."

"She isn't going to like you marrying Ella. Why couldn't you have asked Megan Zehr to marry you? *Mamm* really likes Megan and maybe having her as a daughter-in-law would cheer *mamm* up."

"As much as I love our mother, I'm not going to ask Megan to marry me. Ella is my choice for a wife and everyone is going to have to accept it."

"You're making a mistake, Noah," Gideon grumbled as he began to climb down from the haymow. "You're making a big mistake."

Noah bowed his head and not for the first time that day, asked the Lord for guidance.

Chapter Seventeen

Ella walked across the family room of Susan's tiny house and gave her a hug. "It's so *gut* to see you up and about."

Susan gazed down at the sleeping infant in her arms and stroked his cheek. "There hasn't been much time to rest since these two have been born, but I'm not complaining."

Ella leaned over and kissed her nephew's cheek. "He's so sweet. I can't believe how much he has grown."

"*Jah,*" Susan smiled, "they both have."

Susan's mother walked in carrying baby Grace. "These two keep us on our toes, that's for sure."

Mamm reached to take the *boppli* from her. "*Jah*, I bet they do. I remember how much work it was to have one little one at a time, I can't imagine having two."

Corrine peeked at her niece. "I can't wait until I have *bopplies* of my own."

Mamm laughed. "I think it will be a little while before that happens."

Everyone laughed.

Ella noticed at the mention of babies, Faith frowned and held her stomach. She caught Holly's eye then tilted her head in the direction of their younger sister.

Holly glanced at Faith then raised her eyebrows. She looked back at Ella with a question in her eyes.

Ella shrugged. She didn't know what was wrong with their sister, but she prayed it wasn't what she suspected. Faith had been acting strange lately and it was difficult not to notice that she had been sick several mornings in a row.

"Where are my beautiful grandchildren?" Abram Graber walked in the room wearing a big grin. He took baby Grace out of his wife's arms and then began to croon a lullaby.

"My goodness, Abram. One would think you have never seen a *boppli* before," *Mamm* scolded, but everyone could tell she was pleased.

Susan lowered a sleeping baby Isaac into the bassinet at her feet. "I have something I want to tell all of you. I know I said that I planned to move to Kentucky, but I have decided to stay."

"Oh, Susan, that's wonderful." *Mamm* crossed the room to hug her daughter-in-law. "What made you change your mind?"

"I decided I couldn't move away from my home. I want my children to grow up in LaGrange County, the same place I grew up."

"We will come over every day to help you," *Mamm* promised.

"Well, that is what I wanted to talk to you about." Susan looked at both her in-laws. "Amos Yoder has already rented this house to another family, so my *bopplies* and I will soon not have a place to stay."

Mamm clapped her hands. "You can stay in the downstairs bedroom. We are only using it for storage."

Abram cleared his throat. "Well, that might be okay for now, but soon she will need more room. Come spring, we could add an addition on to the house that will give Susan and the *bopplies* plenty of space."

"Oh, but I couldn't ask you to g[o to] trouble." Susan's eyes watered.

"It wouldn't be any trouble." [she spoke] through tears of her own. "We welcome the chance to have you and the babies stay with us."

"*Danke.*" Susan wiped a tear from her cheek. "My *mamm* and *daed* are disappointed I'm not moving to Kentucky, but I'm sure they will visit often."

"*Jah,* we will." Lizzie came over to sit by her daughter. "The *menner* are in the kitchen discussing plans for the new addition. Your father plans to make a trip back up here in the spring to help."

"You are welcome to stay with us." *Mamm* offered. "I'm sure the men will be working night and day on the addition so it will give us plenty of time to visit."

looked in Faith's direction. Her sister was
holding her stomach again and was staying as far
away as she could from the *bopplies.* She made a
mental note to speak to Faith as soon as they
returned home.

She closed her eyes. *Dear Lord,* she silently
prayed. *Please give me the words to speak to my
little sister.* She opened her eyes and her favorite
Psalm came to mind.

*I will instruct you and teach you in the way you
should go; I will counsel you with my eye upon
you.*

Chapter Eighteen

Ella gave a sharp knock on Faith's bedroom door, then opened it before she could answer. She found her sister sitting on her bed looking at a baby quilt Grandmother Graber had made for her before she was born.

Ella walked over to sit beside her. "Are you feeling okay?"

Faith folded the quilt then got up to put it back in her keepsake box. "*Jah.* I'm fine. Why?"

"I noticed you holding your stomach at Susan's and thought you might not be feeling well."

"Well, you don't have to worry. I'm perfectly fine." Faith walked over to look out the window.

"Is Gideon stopping by this evening?" Ella crossed the room to stand beside her sister. Looking down she noticed a tipped over trash can by Faith's dresser and bent down to set it upright. Her fingers closed around a piece of trash that had fallen out of the can. She stared down at the object in her hand and her stomach plummeted. There was no mistaking the piece of plastic for anything other than a pregnancy test. Nor could Ella deny the positive sign on the object's surface.

"*Jah,* he is," Faith said, then noticed what Ella held in her hand. "Give me that!" She grabbed the pregnancy test.

"Faith," Ella said slowly. "We need to talk."

"*Nee.* We don't!" she snapped. "I just wish you would mind your own business."

"Faith...you're pregnant."

Faith rolled her eyes. "*Jah.* I know. I took the test, remember?"

"Sometimes the tests aren't accurate. Maybe you should take another."

Faith sighed. "I took three of them and they were all positive."

Ella's heart sank. "Oh, Faith," she whispered. "I just wish you would have talked to me first."

"You weren't here," Faith said in a small voice. "You've only been back for a few weeks."

Her sister's look of anguish only fueled her guilt as she sat on the edge of the bed and struggled to find the right words to say. "Is Gideon the father?"

"Of course he's the father!" Faith whispered angrily. "I can't believe you would ask such a question."

"Have you told him?"

Faith shook her head. *"Nee.* I'm going to tell him tonight." She fidgeted with her apron. "He isn't going to be happy."

Ella gave her a hug. "I'm sure he isn't, but he needs to know."

Faith shook her head sadly. "He said he never wanted to have children."

Ella gave a start of surprise. Family was important to the Amish and most wished to marry and have as many children as the Lord provided. "I'm sure Gideon will change his mind over time."

"*Nee.* He won't." Faith jumped at the sound of a buggy pulling up outside. She glanced out the window. "He's here. I have to go."

"Faith," Ella called, before her sister could disappear. "We still need to talk and decide what you are going to do." She moved to follow Faith out of the room. "Plus, you need to tell *mamm* and *daed.*"

Faith hesitated at the top of the stairs. "You won't tell them, will you?"

Ella gave her sister a level look. "I can't make any promises. If you don't tell them, I will. Besides, you aren't going to be able to hide your pregnancy forever."

Faith sighed as if the weight of the world sat upon her shoulders. *"Jah.* I know."

The rest of the evening past in a haze. Ella was quiet during dinner, only speaking when spoken to and then only offering an answer of two or three words. She helped her sisters with the dinner dishes and then spent the rest of the evening sitting and worrying at the kitchen table. It was past eleven o'clock when she heard Faith open the porch door.

Faith stepped into the dimly lit kitchen and then stopped in surprise. "What are you doing up?"

Ella frowned. "I don't know how you think I could possibly sleep after learning of your news."

"*Jah,* well, you shouldn't worry about me." Faith shrugged. "I spoke with Gideon and everything is going to be fine."

"Did he offer to marry you?"

Anger flashed in Faith's eyes. "*Nee,* he didn't, but he has a solution to our problem."

Ella was beginning to worry. A baby was a blessing, not a problem. She hoped Faith wasn't planning on doing something she would later regret.

"When are you going to tell *mamm* and *daed*?"

Faith's eyes narrowed. "Soon. I don't want to tell them before I'm ready."

"Faith, they're going to find out."

"*Jah,* they will," she said as she headed for the stairs, "but hopefully by then, things will be different."

That was what Ella was worried about. She sat up late into the night thinking about Faith, the baby and how everyone's world was about to change.

Chapter Nineteen

Church Sunday dawned crisp and clear. Ella slipped out of bed, quickly dressed and headed downstairs to help her mother with breakfast.

Her mother greeted her as she walked into the kitchen. "Good morning, Ella. How are you on this fine day the Lord has given us?"

"Good morning, *mamm*." She poured herself a cup of *kaffi* then began to set the table for breakfast.

Holly gave her a nudge. "Did you speak to Faith?" she whispered.

"*Jah,* I did."

"And?"

"I'll tell you later," Ella said softly.

"Something worrying you, daughter?" her father asked as he came in from outside."

Ella took a deep breath. *"Jah,* there is."

Faith placed the butter and jam on the table and gave Ella a dark look. "Ella. You promised," she hissed.

Ella looked her sister in the eye. "They need to know."

"All right, you two." Their father motioned for them to have a seat at the table. "Start talking."

Ella glanced at Faith. "Do you want to tell them, or should I?"

"Be my guest!" Faith snapped. "You've already butted in where you don't belong."

"Faith." Their mother admonished.

"I will tell you what's wrong, but I don't want Corrine to hear." Faith cast a worried glance at her younger sister who was listening intently.

"Corrine." *Daed* motioned toward the stairs.
"Please go up to your room. We will call you
when it's time to come down."

Corrine made a face but quickly did as she was
told.

"Vell?" Their father looked at both of them
with a frown. "Do you mind telling me what's
going on? I won't tolerate bickering in my
house."

Ella waited for Faith to speak, but Faith only
folded her arms and stared at the surface of the
table.

"Faith is pregnant," Ella whispered, the words
feeling like sawdust in her throat.

"Faith?" *Mamm* cried. "Is that true?"

"Jah," Faith mumbled. She shot Ella an angry
look.

Their father sat for a moment without speaking, then he got up and walked out of the house.

Holly shook her head as she gave Ella a surprised look. "Why didn't you tell me?" she whispered.

Their mother jumped up from the table. "We can talk about this later," she said briskly. "Right now we need to finish breakfast or we will be late for church."

The ride to church was a solemn one. Ella breathed a sigh of relief when their father turned the buggy into the Beiler's driveway.

She was greeted at the buggy by her good friend, Becky Glick. Becky was married to Matthew and they had been married for five years and had a two-year-old daughter, a one-year-old son and a *boppli* on the way.

"Ella!" Becky gave her a hug. "It's so wonderful to see you. My mother told me you moved back home."

"Who are these precious children?" Ella crouched down and smiled at the toddlers who were clinging to their mother's skirt.

"This is our daughter, Johanna." Becky put her hand on the head of the blonde little girl. "And this is our son, Jacob." She pulled her young son forward.

"Such beautiful children, Becky. You and Matthew must be extremely happy."

Becky gave a soft smile. "We have been blessed, *jah.*" She placed a hand on her stomach. "And this little one is due in four months."

Ella gazed wistfully at her friend's children. Would she and Noah have been married and had children if she had never left?

Becky patted her on the shoulder. "I'm sorry I couldn't come to Isaac's funeral. I was in Pennsylvania visiting my sister, Hattie and her family."

Ella nodded in understanding. "It was a sad day to be sure, but the Lord brought us through it."

Becky shifted uncomfortably. "I don't mean to pry, but how are things between you and Noah? Have you seen him much since you've been back home?"

Ella smiled. "*Jah,* I have. We seem to be getting along just fine."

Becky breathed a sigh of relief. *"Gut.* I'm happy to hear it. I know Noah to be a fair and honest man. I didn't think he would treat you unkindly, because of the accident."

Ella laughed as they joined the line of women and young girls filing into the Beiler's barn for church service. "*Nee,* far from it."

Once inside, she took a seat on the backless bench next to Holly and Faith. Faith kept her head down and didn't bother to look across the room at Gideon, who was desperately trying to catch her eye. Ella gave him a stern look and the young man flushed and looked away.

Soon the congregations' voices were joined in praise as they sang hymns from the Ausbund. Ella closed her eyes and felt her spirit soar as she was wrapped in the comforting songs that had been sung by generations before her.

Before long, the singing was over and one of the ministers stood to deliver the first sermon. Ella's eyes opened in shock as a familiar deep voice washed over her and her gaze flew to the front of the room.

Noah met her gaze and nodded as he continued to preach.

Ella had forgotten that Noah was a minister and could still get in trouble for dating her before she became a baptized member of the church. She was still contemplating this fact a few minutes later when the congregation knelt for silent prayer. She prayed for the Lord to help Faith and Gideon make the right decisions and for her parents to come to terms with Faith's pregnancy. Last, she prayed for the Lord's guidance in her relationship with Noah.

After the main sermon, the congregation rose to begin their various duties. The men began to assemble the backless benches into tables for the noon meal, while the women readied the food to be served.

Ella fell into step beside Faith who was looking ill. "Are you feeling okay?" she whispered as she smiled and nodded to members of the congregation.

"I would have felt better if you hadn't told *mamm* and *daed."* Faith gave her a sour look.

"I'm sorry, but it couldn't be helped." Ella picked up a platter of peanut butter marshmallow fluff sandwiches and prepared to serve the men who were already seated.

"Whatever." Faith grabbed a pot of coffee and followed her.

Ella turned to her sister. "We will talk about this more at home, *jah?"*

"*Jah,"* Faith grumbled.

Noah smiled at Ella when she served him a sandwich and she found herself looking away, afraid her expression would convey her feelings of love for the entire congregation to see.

The rest of the afternoon passed in a blur. Ella did her best to smile and chat with family and friends, but her mind was preoccupied with Faith, Gideon and the baby that would be born in a few months.

Ella knew when *daed* sent Corrine home with Uncle Melvin and Aunt Ada, that there would be a serious discussion once they returned home. He waited until they were all seated in the parlor before facing Faith with barely controlled anger.

"You are not allowed to see that boy again!" He shook his finger an inch from Faith's nose. "Ever since his father died, Gideon has been allowed to run wild."

Ella shrank back into the couch. Their father was usually mild mannered and easy going, but Faith's behavior had pushed his patience to the limit.

"Abram…" *Mamm* placed a calming hand on *Daed's* arm.

"Let me handle this, Gretta."

Their father shook his head sadly as his anger abated. "You are not permitted to see Gideon Wyse until we speak with the Bishop. I expect the two of you to be married as soon as possible."

"But, *daed…*" Faith began to sob quietly. "Gideon doesn't want to get married."

Their father's look was thunderous. "This afternoon, your mother and I will speak with Martha Wyse about her son."

Faith jumped up and ran from the room. They could hear her loud footsteps on the stairs, then the slamming of her bedroom door.

Daed turned to Ella. "I will be speaking to Noah, as well. As a minister of the church, he should have monitored his younger brother's behavior a little more closely."

"*Jah, daed.*"

A scripture came to mind as she walked out of the room.

My help comes from the Lord, who made heaven and earth.

Chapter Twenty

"Speak to me, Ella." Noah sat on the porch swing and regarded her with a look of concern.

With bleak eyes, she said, "Faith is pregnant."

Noah gave a start of surprise. "Do you think Gideon is the father?"

"*Jah.*"

Noah removed his hat and ran a hand through his thick hair. He was quiet for a moment, lost in thought as he stared across the yard with unseeing eyes.

He turned to face her. "But you cannot be sure, can you?"

Ella felt a flash of anger, but willed herself to remain calm. "Of course I'm sure. Faith says that Gideon is the father of the baby and I believe her."

Noah remained motionless beside her. Ella rose to walk to the porch railing, looking out over the winter landscape. The whole thing seemed part of a dream and any moment she would awaken to a world where Faith wasn't pregnant and Isaac was still alive to parent his young *bopplies.*

Noah came over to stand beside her. "I will speak with Gideon."

"Danke."

He enfolded her in his arms and murmured, "If Gideon is the father of the baby I will not allow him to shirk his responsibility."

Ella bristled and took a step back. "What do you mean *if* he is the father?"

Noah tucked his hands into his pockets and sighed. "Ella, this is my *bruder* we are talking about. I need to speak with him before I form an opinion."

Her chin lifted. "Then I guess we have nothing left to say." She turned and went inside, slamming the door behind her.

Her mother looked up from the meal preparations. "Is that Noah I see leaving?"

Ella nodded as she got the ingredients out of the cupboard to make biscuits.

"I thought he planned to stay for dinner?" *Mamm* placed a pan of chicken in the oven then turned to regard her with a question in her eyes.

Ella shrugged. "I guess he decided to go home."

Mamm lifted her brows. "Did the two of you have an argument?"

She nodded. "I told him Faith is pregnant."

"Oh, Ella." Her mother gave her a look of disapproval. "Your father isn't going to be happy you spoke to Noah. He planned to talk the matter over with him tonight after dinner."

"*Jah,* well, Noah is questioning whether or not Gideon is the father of Faith's baby."

Her mother gasped. "He can't possibly think Faith is the kind of girl who dates lots of boys!"

"*Nee.*" Ella knew what her mother was implying even though she left the words unspoken. "He doesn't think anything of the sort. He needs time to digest the information."

A short time later they sat down to a dinner of baked chicken, biscuits, mounds of fluffy mashed potatoes and green beans. Faith was noticeably absent having complained of a headache and retired early.

Their father cleared his throat. "Tomorrow we are helping Susan and the *bopplies* move."

Corrine's face brightened and she clapped her hands. "I can't wait for Susan and the *bopplies* to live here. It will be so much fun."

"*Jah,*" Holly agreed. "There will be a lot of changes, but I know it will be *gut* for them to live here at the farm."

"Susan has most of her things packed," *Mamm* said as she got up to serve a dessert of angel food cake. "I will go over in the morning and begin to bring over some of her boxes."

"Their father leaned back in his chair. "Several of the men from church have volunteered to help move Susan's furniture. We will set her bed and cribs up in the spare bedroom and store the rest of the furniture in the shed."

That night after *daed* read scripture from the Bible, Ella climbed the stairs to her room. Moonlight streamed through the bedroom window creating a hazy pattern on the floor. She watched as dark clouds scuttled across the moon's surface and she knew that it would rain soon.

She shivered as she climbed into bed, a sense of foreboding wrapping her in its cold embrace.

"Ella?" Holly whispered from her side of the room.

"*Jah?*"

"Do you think we should check on Faith?"

Their younger sister had been ensconced in her room all evening, declining to participate in the family devotionals and ignoring their repeated pleas for her to come downstairs.

"Nee. Maybe we should let Faith have this time alone."

"Do you think she and Gideon will marry?"

Ella couldn't picture the self-centered Gideon Wyse being a husband nor a father, but she didn't wish to voice her opinion.

"I don't know." Ella sighed. "I'm fairly certain neither one of them are ready to be parents, but the baby will be here in a few months whether they are ready or not."

"Well, at least Susan's *bopplies* will have a cousin close to their age," Holly said, always looking on the bright side.

"Jah, they will," Ella murmured as her eyelids grew heavy. She said a prayer for the Lord to bless the soon to be young family.

The wind whistled and moaned, buffeting the tree outside their bedroom window. Ella closed her eyes and drifted off to sleep.

Chapter Twenty-one

Lightening flashed, illuminating the night sky, followed by a loud boom of thunder. Faith eased open the barn door and hurried inside as droplets of rain began to pelt the earth.

"Gideon?" She peered into the shadows as she clutched her cloak around her, a hand resting protectively on her stomach.

"Over here." A rustling came from her right and Gideon emerged from the thick blanket of darkness. "I was beginning to think you weren't coming."

Faith ran to give him a hug and was relieved when his arms closed around her, wrapping her and their unborn child in his embrace.

"I had to wait for everyone to fall asleep." Faith let Gideon lead her over to a hay bale. She took a seat and waited for him to join her, but he remained standing.

"Have you been here long?" Faith squinted her eyes at the figure in front of her, but Gideon was once again cloaked in shadows.

"A little over an hour." His rough voice came from the left. "I was getting ready to leave."

Faith placed her hand on her stomach again as she felt the baby kick. Their unborn child had become more active as her pregnancy progressed. Soon, she would no longer be able to hide her condition underneath the heavy bulk of winter clothing and the entire community would know her shame.

"I'm happy you didn't. We have a lot to talk about."

"I don't know what you want from me." Gideon's voice was harsh. "Noah spent the entire evening pressuring me to take responsibility for my actions. He wants me to speak to Bishop Burkholder."

"And?" Faith held her breath. For the first time since she had learned she was pregnant, hope flared. Maybe things would work out after all. She and Gideon would marry and provide a home for their child. There might be some talk in the beginning when a baby arrived so soon after the vows had been spoken, but given time, the gossip would cease.

"And, what?" Gideon growled in her ear as he took a seat next to her. "I don't want to get married. I'm way too young to be tied down and getting married would ruin the plans I have for my life."

Faith felt panic set in as she struggled to make sense of Gideon's words.

"I...I don't understand. How am I to raise a child? You promised you had a plan and everything would work out in the end." Her words ended on a sob.

Gideon gave a bark of laughter. "I meant everything will work out for *me*. I've already spoken to Levi Hochstetler and he said I could stay with him until I find a place of my own."

Faith remembered Levi Hochstetler. He had been wild and outspoken and had gone out of his way to break the community's rules until he had left last summer. Nothing good would come out of Gideon hanging around Levi for any length of time.

Faith grasped his arm. "But what about me? You can't leave me to face this on my own."

Gideon sighed. "You won't be all alone. I'm sure your parents and sisters will help with the *boppli*."

"What will everyone in the community think?" Faith choked back a sob. "Remember how people acted last year when Tricia Schwartz became pregnant without being married?"

"*Jah,* I do," Gideon whispered, "but things might be different for you. Your family is well respected in the community."

"Gideon. You can't leave me." Faith was crying freely now. "The baby needs a father."

"Faith," he said through gritted teeth, "for the last time, I'm not ready to take on that kind of responsibility."

He got up and began to pace. "I plan to leave in a few days. Levi said he would drive out to pick me up Friday night. I just need to wait for him a half mile from my home underneath the big maple tree."

Faith knew the tree he was talking about. She and Gideon had often met there after she had crept out of the house in the middle of the night.

She jumped to her feet. "I can go with you!"

Gideon stopped pacing. "I'm going to be staying with Levi and several of his roommates. I don't think it would be a *gut* idea for you to room with a bunch of guys."

"Please, Gideon?" Faith hated the pleading note in her voice, but she couldn't let him leave without her.

"Faith…"

Faith reached for him. "Can't we stay with them for a little while until we get a place of our own? I could get a job waiting tables to help pay the bills. It could work, Gideon, we could be a family."

"But I don't want a family," he snapped.

Faith sat back down before her knees gave out. "But, I love you," she whispered, "and I love our baby."

Gideon sat down and wrapped his arms around her, but didn't return her words of love. "Neither one of us is ready to raise a child."

"You might change your mind once the baby is born."

"I won't."

"Can I come with you when you leave? I wouldn't have to stay with you. I could find a place of my own." Unshed tears trembled on Faith's lashes as she held on to a flicker of hope.

Gideon sighed. "You would have to be ready to leave this Friday. If you don't show up at the maple tree by midnight, I'm leaving without you."

Faith rose to her feet. "I'll be there. I promise." She gave Gideon a quick kiss on the cheek and slipped out the door into the rainy night.

Chapter Twenty-two

Susan's moving day was rainy and cold. Ella sat in the kitchen holding baby Isaac and watched through the window as men from their community unloaded Susan's furniture from several wagons. They placed most of the furniture in the shed, only bringing Susan's bed and the cribs inside.

Ella placed a kiss on top of her nephew's downy head. She was surprised at how much he resembled her brother even at this young age.

Noah walked through the kitchen preparing to go outside for another load of items from her mother's buggy. *Mamm* had made two trips this morning bringing over all of Susan's things that were packed in boxes.

Noah paused in the doorway. "Ella? Could we talk for a minute after I finish unloading your mother's buggy?"

"Jah," Ella said, hoping he had some solution to Faith and Gideon's dilemma.

"Gut." Noah nodded before heading back outside into the pouring rain.

Susan walked into the kitchen holding Grace. "I can't believe how much it has rained since yesterday. I feel sorry for the men moving my furniture, it can't be an easy job in the cold and the wet."

Mamm caught the tail end of Susan's sentence as she hustled into the kitchen. *"Jah,* the *menner* are going to need some hot coffee, that's for sure." She placed a coffee pot filled with water on the stove.

"*Danke,* again for allowing us to stay here," Susan said softly. "I'm not sure what the babies and I would have done otherwise."

Mamm walked over to give her daughter-in-law a hug. "Abram and I wouldn't have it any other way. There's no need to thank us. This is your home now."

Grandmother Graber walked in from the *dawdi haus* carrying a tray of cookies. "It's about time to fix lunch, don't you think? The men must be getting hungry after working so hard."

"*Jah,*" Holly said as she walked into the kitchen. "We need to begin making sandwiches."

"Holly, you can start fixing ham sandwiches," their mother said, "while I finish heating up the chicken and noodles I made last night." She bent down to pull a tray of freshly made rolls out of the oven. "There are mashed potatoes in the pan on the stove."

Corrine walked over to Ella and looked down at her nephew. "Can I hold him?"

"*Jah,*" Ella got up from her chair, "you can. Do you want to sit in the chair by the wood stove?"

Corrine nodded as she hastily climbed into the chair and held out her arms for the precious bundle. "You're so cute," she murmured to baby Isaac as she began to sing him a soft lullaby.

"Where is Faith?" Holly whispered as the men came in for lunch.

Ella shrugged. "She's probably pouting in her room."

Noah caught her eye as he walked in the door. He nodded toward the porch and then waited for her to follow.

Ella wrapped her sweater around her as she joined Noah on the rain swept porch. She sat down next to him on the swing.

"You should be eating lunch, don't you think?" She gave him a soft smile.

"I'll eat in a minute, but right now, we need to talk."

"Did you speak to Gideon?"

"Jah." Noah sighed. "I'm afraid it didn't do much good."

Ella was shocked. She knew Gideon was self-centered, but he had always listened to his older brother.

"Noah, please tell me he plans to marry Faith and take responsibility for the baby?"

"Nee, he doesn't." Noah's voice was low. "I just want you to know, Faith doesn't have to

handle this on her own. I will help support the baby."

"Oh, Noah." Ella's heart filled with even more love for the man sitting beside her. "You shouldn't have to carry your brother's burdens."

Noah sighed. "I've neglected Gideon. He needed a father figure after *daed* died and I'm afraid I let him down. I was so immersed in my own grief, I couldn't see my little brother was suffering. Now, I'm afraid it's too late."

"I'm sure you did the best you could. You can't blame yourself for Gideon's actions. He is old enough to know right from wrong."

Ella's mother poked her head out the door and gave them a questioning look. "If the two of you want to eat, you need to come inside before all the food is gone."

They both rose to go back inside the house.

Noah paused. "I'm sorry I couldn't have given you better news. Gideon is determined to charge headfirst down the wrong path and I can't do much to stop him."

"You aren't responsible for your brother's actions. Hopefully, one day, he will see the error of his ways and decide to do what is best for Faith and the baby. We can only pray that he comes to that decision soon."

"*Jah,*" Noah agreed before they stepped inside, "that, we can do."

Once inside the kitchen, they both filled their plates and sat down at the table.

Ella's father walked past and clapped Noah on the shoulder. "How are the renovations going on your property?"

Noah's face relaxed. "*Gut.* I've managed to replace the flooring in the kitchen and refinish the cabinets. I still have a lot of painting to do, though."

Abram rubbed his bearded jaw. "Well, now, if it's alright with you, I can close the shop tomorrow and we can see what else needs to be done around your place."

Noah smiled. "I would welcome the help, but you don't need to close the shop. What remains to be done can be finished over time."

Abram waved away his protest. "It wouldn't be a problem. We are caught up on orders, so now would be the perfect time to get things done around your place. Besides," he winked, "I have a feeling you might want to get things finished sooner rather than later."

Ella flushed as her father chuckled and moved away. She glanced at Noah and saw that his ears were pink.

"Noah?" Ella's mother handed him a plate of cookies covered in plastic wrap. "Why don't you take these home for Luke?"

"*Danke.* I'm sure Luke will enjoy the treat."

After everyone had left, Ella turned to her mother. "Did Faith come downstairs to eat?"

"*Nee.*" Her mother filled the sink with sudsy water in preparation to wash the dishes.

"Maybe we should take some food up to her?" Ella chewed on her lower lip.

"*Nee!* If your sister wants to eat, she can come downstairs like the rest of us." *Mamm* placed a stack of dishes in the sink harder than necessary causing water to slosh over the sides. "I won't have your sister being babied, because of her condition."

"What condition?" Corrine asked, as she walked in the kitchen and grabbed a cookie.

"The asking too many questions one," *Mamm* replied, as she shooed her youngest daughter out of the kitchen. "And it seems to be catching."

Ella faced her mother. "Corrine is going to find out about Faith's pregnancy. You can't keep it a secret forever."

Her mother arched her brows. "Well, she doesn't have to find out about it today."

That night as they lay in bed, Holly whispered, "Ella?"

"*Jah?*"

Did you see Faith at all today?"

"*Nee,* I didn't."

Holly sighed. "I think I heard her crying this afternoon."

"Well," Ella said slowly, "I'm sure her situation is upsetting. It must be scary to be facing motherhood alone."

"She isn't alone. She has us."

"*Jah,* but it isn't the same as having a supportive husband by your side."

"*Nee,*" Holly sighed, as she burrowed further under her covers, "but I'm sure Gideon will change his mind once the baby is born."

Ella wasn't so sure, but she said a prayer for God to work on Gideon's heart as she drifted off to sleep.

Chapter Twenty-three

The bright spring sun beamed down from the blue sky as Ella and Faith walked through the south field, picking up sticks and branches that had fallen during the recent thunderstorm.

Faith placed a hand on the growing child in her stomach as she bent over to pick up a tree limb and groaned.

"Ach, Faith, you shouldn't be lifting such heavy things," Ella exclaimed, as she rushed over to relieve her sister of her burden. "You need to think about the baby."

"I am thinking about the baby!" Faith snapped. "All I do is think about the baby and what a mess I've made of my life."

Ella sat down underneath a tree lining the fence row and motioned for Faith to take a seat beside her. "You and Gideon made a mistake, *jah,* but the baby is a blessing from God."

Faith stared off into the distance, her eyes troubled. "I'm not so sure it's a blessing."

"You can't mean that."

"I do mean it. This baby is causing nothing, but trouble. Gideon blames me and I'm afraid I might lose him." Her lower lip trembled. "I thought having a baby would force Gideon to marry me."

"Faith," Ella said slowly, as her stomach sank. "You didn't get pregnant on purpose, did you?"

A tear trickled down Faith's cheek. "I just wanted Gideon to ask me to marry him, that's all. I was so certain he would after he learned I was pregnant, but that hasn't been the case."

Ella's heart ached for her younger sister. How misguided she had been and now an innocent child would have to pay for its mother's mistake.

She knew it wasn't uncommon for girl's to intentionally become pregnant in order to try and hang on to a boyfriend, but it wasn't something that typically happened in the Amish community.

"Gideon still needs to take responsibility for the baby." Ella smoothed her hands over her skirt. "You didn't get pregnant on your own."

"*Nee,* but Gideon says that a baby isn't in his plans." Faith's tone was bitter. "He doesn't want a family."

"Well, it's a little late for that, don't you think?" Ella huffed. "Gideon needs to step up to the plate and shoulder some of the responsibility instead of gallivanting around with his friends like he doesn't have a care in the world."

"Step up to the plate?" Faith gave a faint smile. "Sometimes you sound so *Englisch.*"

"Well, I did live out in the world for six years, so it's to be expected."

They rose and began the long trek back to the house.

"Do you miss it?" Faith nibbled on a blade of grass as they walked.

Ella pondered the question for a moment. *"Nee,* I don't, everything I want in life is here."

"You mean, Noah?"

Ella blushed. *"Jah,* Noah is important to me, but so are all of you. I can't imagine leaving my family again."

Faith sighed. "I wish Gideon was more like Noah."

Ella nodded. "Well, to be fair, Noah is a good deal older than Gideon. I'm not sure how Noah would have acted if he had been faced with the same situation when he was eighteen."

"Weren't you dating Noah when he was eighteen?"

Ella laughed. *"Nee,* I wasn't. I was only fourteen at the time."

"Oh, right." Faith giggled. "I sometimes forget the two of you aren't the same age."

They neared the house and noticed a buggy parked out front.

"Isn't that Megan Zehr's buggy?" Faith asked as they walked closer.

"I wouldn't know," Ella said, as they walked past. She hoped Faith was wrong. She was in no mood to be polite to Noah's former girlfriend.

"Ella?" their mother said, with a strained look as they entered the kitchen. "Megan has stopped by to see you."

"Wonderful," Ella mumbled under her breath. To Megan, she said, "Would you like a cup of *kaffi?*"

"Thank you." Megan's smile was fleeting. "I would love a cup of coffee."

"Girls." *Mamm* motioned to Faith and Holly. "We need to get started on the laundry." The three of them filed out and left Megan and Ella alone.

"I brought over some lemon bars." Megan motioned to a tray on the table. "I remembered your grandmother saying they were her favorite."

"Danke." Ella took a seat at the table. "I'm sure if my grandmother were here, she would appreciate them. She and my grandfather had to go to Ohio to attend a funeral."

"Oh," Megan's face fell. "Well, I'll be sure to bring over some more once she returns. Your grandmother was a big help to me in the weeks after I lost Josephus. She would come over most mornings to help with the children, to clean, or to just sit and talk. I will be forever grateful for her support."

"It is *gut* she was able to help you. I'm sure your family was a big help as well."

"*Jah,* Josephus's family helped a lot." Megan fell silent as she stared out the window.

"What about your own family?"

Megan turned to her, her gaze cool. "I have no family."

Ella was shocked. She couldn't imagine what it would be like not to have family. Even during the years she had been gone, she had known that her family was here, waiting for her to come back home.

"No one?"

Megan sighed. *"Nee.* My parents were abusive and I was taken away from them at age three and placed in foster care."

"I'm sorry," Ella whispered. Several of her former students had been in the foster care system and she would never forget the lost and haunted looks in some of the children's eyes.

"Megan shrugged. "It's all water under the bridge."

"It couldn't have been an easy way to grow up."

"Nee, it wasn't pleasant, but I survived."

Ella didn't want to pry, but she was curious as to why Megan wasn't still close to her foster family. "What happened to your foster family?"

Megan's mouth tightened. "I didn't have just one foster family. I was bounced from home to home from the age of three until I turned eighteen."

Ella was stunned. "Megan, I'm so sorry. I didn't realize what you had gone through. We don't have to continue talking about it if you don't want to."

Megan gave a faint smile. "Don't worry. It feels like it happened a lifetime ago, but maybe it will explain why family and community are so precious to me."

Ella returned the smile. "I saw you at church on Sunday. Your children are wonderful."

"*Danke.*" Megan laughed. "I would say Carmen and Nathaniel are a lot like me, but they actually take after their father."

"I remember Josephus from school. I was saddened when I learned of his passing."

Megan's eyes filled with tears. "There isn't a day that goes by that I don't miss him. I hear his laugh when Nathaniel finds something funny or see his smile when Carmen grins, but it is getting easier. Time heals all wounds, *jah?*"

Ella got up to place her coffee mug in the sink. "I'm sure Susan could tell you more about that than me."

"How is Susan?"

"She is taking one day at a time. It's *gut* to have her and the twins living here."

Megan nodded. "*Jah,* family is important." She hesitated. "Ella...there is something I need to tell you."

Ella became swamped with fear. Had Megan come over to tell her something about Noah?

"*Jah?*"

Megan smiled. "Please don't be worried. I came over to tell you that you shouldn't be concerned about my relationship with Noah. We are friends, nothing more. The only woman he has eyes for is you."

"Really?" Even though Noah had asked her to marry him, she couldn't shake the jealousy she felt over Megan and Noah's close friendship.

Megan chuckled. *"Jah,* lately you are all he can talk about and I just wanted to let you know that I'm happy for the two of you."

Ella's eyes widened. "You are?"

"Jah, I am. The two of you belong together, anyone can see that."

"Thank you, for telling me, Megan."

Megan rose from her chair. "You're welcome. Now, I really must be going. A neighbor was kind enough to watch Carmen and Nathaniel, but I need to get home and fix them lunch."

Ella escorted her to the door. "It was *gut* to see you, Megan. Please feel free to stop by anytime and next time you are welcome to bring your children."

Megan smiled. "Thank you, Ella. I have a feeling we are going to be *gut* friends."

"*Jah,*" Ella agreed. "I think so too."

That night, Ella said a prayer for Megan and their new friendship.

Chapter Twenty-four

It was late Friday evening when Faith eased open the porch door and crept out into the moonlit night. In her hand she carried a small suitcase with all the *Englisch* clothes she owned. These clothes had been hidden in a box underneath her bed. If her parents had known she was secretly wearing *Englisch* clothes when she went out with her friends, they would have forbidden it.

She paused to glance up at the second story, wishing she could tell her sisters goodbye. She didn't know how long it would be before she saw them again, but it would be after the baby was born.

As she walked, Faith's thoughts were on Gideon, their baby and the life they would build together. Maybe when they were on their own, away from the confines of the community, they would unite and lean on each other for support as they navigated their strange, new world.

Lost in thought, she didn't see Gideon until he stepped out of the night's shadows.

"I thought you had changed your mind." Gideon didn't look pleased to see her. He reached to take the suitcase out of her hand.

"I had to wait until everyone went to sleep. *Mamm* and *daed* stayed up late talking."

"You shouldn't have come, Faith," Gideon sighed. "Levi said you can only stay with us for a couple of weeks, then you have to find a place of your own."

"You mean *we* have to find a place of our own?"

"Nee," Gideon said as a car pulled up in front of them. "I'm still going to live with Levi and his roommates. You are going to have to find a place for yourself."

Levi rolled down the car window. "Are the two of you coming or not?"

Stunned, Faith climbed into the backseat of the car. She had been so sure that Gideon would change his mind about their living arrangements. Instead, he seemed happy to start a life without her. She could feel her dreams of creating a happy, little family fade away as the car rolled forward and they disappeared into the night.

Mamm frowned as she began breakfast preparations. Most of her daughters were helping in the kitchen, but Faith was noticeably absent.

She turned to Corrine who was busy setting the table. "Corrine, could you please go upstairs and hurry your sister along?

"*Jah, Mamm.*" Corrine set down the silverware she was holding and ran to the stairs.

Holly looked at Ella. "I wonder if Faith is having more morning sickness?" she whispered. "She has been sick every morning this week."

"*Jah,* she has." Ella was worried about her younger sister. She had read that morning sickness was supposed to dissipate during the first trimester and Faith was further along than that.

"*Mamm! Daed!*" Corrine thundered down the stairs a minute later.

"Goodness, Corrine," their mother scolded. "If you don't quiet down you will wake the *bopplies.*"

"Don't worry," Susan said, as she walked into the room holding Grace. "This little one has been awake for hours." She placed Grace in a travel crib in the corner and left to get Isaac.

"Mamm," Corrine wheezed. "Faith is gone."

"Oh, Corrine." Their mother placed a platter of fried eggs and sausage on the table. "She is probably taking a shower. Go back up, knock on the door and tell her she needs to come down."

"Nee," Corrine shook her head. "She isn't. I already checked."

Their mother sighed as she left the kitchen and climbed the stairs. A few minutes later they all heard her cry. "Abram! Our daughter is gone."

"What on earth is all the fuss about?" Their father walked in from outside.

"Faith is gone." Tears filled their mother's eyes as she walked back into the kitchen.

Their father's face paled. "Are you certain? Maybe she got up early and decided to take a walk."

"Nee," Mamm said as she sagged into his arms. "She is really gone, Abram. Our pregnant daughter is out in the world with no one to watch over her."

"Faith is pregnant?" Corrine asked, eyes wide.

"Quiet, now," Holly said and motioned for her to take a seat at the table. "Let *mamm* and *daed* talk."

Their father led their mother into the next room. They could hear them talking in hushed voices. A short time later, they came back to the kitchen and sat down to a breakfast that had grown cold.

Daed lowered his head to signal the silent blessing.

Ella prayed for Faith and her unborn child. She knew how difficult it was to live in the *Englisch* world and the obstacles her sister would have to face. It wouldn't be easy for Faith to support herself and a baby.

Their father cleared his throat signaling that prayer time was over. He looked up, his eyes red. "*Vell,* I guess Faith has made her decision. The only thing we can do is keep her in our prayers."

Their mother gasped. "Surely you will look for her? Our daughter needs to be brought home where she belongs."

Daed shook his head. "*Nee,* Gretta. Faith is eighteen. If she wants to move away from home, it's perfectly legal for her to do so. Hopefully, in time, she will decide to come back to us, but it's her decision to make."

Mamm stared at her husband in disbelief. "But, what about the baby? Faith doesn't have a job. She isn't capable of supporting herself and a child."

"Well," their father stroked his chin, "something tells me Faith didn't leave alone. I have a feeling Martha Wyse found her son missing this morning as well. I will take a ride over there in a little while to speak to her."

They heard the sound of a buggy pulling up outside.

Holly jumped up and ran to the window. "Noah just arrived."

Ella got up and ran outside to meet him.

He jumped down from the buggy and turned to her with troubled eyes. "Is Faith…?"

"She's gone," Ella whispered, and stepped into his arms for a hug. "What are we going to do? Faith needs to be here where she can have help with the baby. I can't imagine Gideon supporting her and their child."

Noah sighed and stepped away. "Gideon isn't all bad, Ella. He is a little spoiled, but I'm certain he will take care of Faith and the baby. Why would he have allowed her to go with him otherwise?"

"Maybe Faith insisted." Ella knew how stubborn her sister could be.

"Even so, I'm sure Gideon will take care of her."

"Will you look for them?"

Noah looked down into her upturned face and nodded. "I plan on speaking with several of his friends. Maybe some of them will have a clue where Gideon and Faith have gone."

"Thank you, Noah."

They both turned at the sound of the porch door opening. Ella's father stepped out onto the porch and motioned to Noah.

Ella sank down on a bench underneath the big maple tree and silently began to pray.

Chapter Twenty-five

Holly turned to Ella as they hung freshly laundered clothes on the line. "Do you think Faith will come back before long?"

Ella sighed. "I don't know, Holly. I think Faith left because of Gideon. If he decides to return and become a baptized member of the community, I'm sure Faith will return with him."

Ella turned as Noah's buggy pulled up beside the house.

"Well?" Ella didn't like the look on Noah's face as he joined them by the clothesline. "Were you able to speak with Gideon's friends?"

"*Jah.*" Noah stared at his feet then raised his dark, blue gaze to capture hers. "If they know where Gideon and Faith have gone, they aren't saying."

Ella gave Noah an anguished look as tears threatened to spill. "What are we going to do? We can't give up looking for them."

Noah removed his straw hat and ran a hand through his hair. "Ella, I'm sorry. I haven't a clue where they have gone. All we can do is pray for the Lord to keep them safe and for their swift return."

"But, Noah…"

Noah shook his head, signaling an end to the conversation. He walked back to his buggy and wearily climbed inside.

Ella stood and watched helplessly as Noah's buggy moved slowly down the lane. She turned to her sister. "I can't believe he is willing to give up on finding them."

"Oh, I don't know," Holly said as she picked up the laundry basket. "Maybe Noah is tired of searching for the ones he loves. He spent months looking for you after you left."

"He did?" Ella had known he had looked for her, but hadn't realized he had searched for her that long.

"*Jah.*" Holly nodded. "Noah was miserable after you left. Not only had he lost his brother and father, he lost you as well. He spent all of his free time talking to your friends and looking for you. He even went to Merrillville to search for you after receiving a tip that you were working in a restaurant there."

Ella froze. She had lived in Merrillville for a brief time while she had earned her GED. Just the thought of Noah searching for her amongst the hustle and bustle of the city, brought tears to her eyes.

"I didn't know," she murmured.

"*Jah,* well, you hurt a lot of people when you left." Her normally pleasant sister regarded her with a hint of anger. "*Mamm* cried for weeks after you left and *Daed* became withdrawn. Now, Faith has followed in your footsteps."

Ella folded her arms. "Our situations are entirely different. I left home because of the accident. Faith left, because of Gideon."

"Doesn't matter." Holly said as she headed toward the house. "You both ran away from your problems. It seems to me the two of you are more alike than you think."

Ella bristled, but couldn't deny the truth in Holly's words. She had run away from her problems and now Faith was following her example.

Their mother was baking pies when they walked in the kitchen. Tears rolled down her cheeks as she silently worked.

"Did Noah have any word about Faith and Gideon?" *Mamm's* voice was heartbroken as she rolled out crust for the pies.

"*Nee.*" Ella sat down at the table. "He said Gideon's friends don't know where they are."

Their mother sighed. "Well, I guess she will come back home when she is ready. We are just going to have to pray over the matter, *jah?*"

Holly and Ella both nodded.

That night, Ella spent extra time in prayer, asking the Lord to help her find peace with Faith's decision. Wrapped in sorrow, she allowed herself to fall asleep, comforted in the knowledge that the Lord was watching over them all.

Chapter Twenty-six

Faith coughed as thick cigarette smoke swirled around her head. From the corner of the room came the sounds of male laughter as Gideon, Levi and his roommates battled it out on the latest video game.

She softly called to Gideon, telling him she was going to turn in for the night. Her only response was a grunt and a wave of his hand in her direction.

Curling up on the double air mattress thrown in a corner of the living room, she placed a hand on her stomach as tears threatened.

This wasn't how she had envisioned things to be. She had pictured spending time with Gideon, leaning on him for support as they faced this new challenge together. Instead, she had been cast aside and all but forgotten as Gideon quickly bonded with Levi and his friends.

Dear, Lord, she silently prayed as the tears began to fall, *please watch over me and my unborn baby. I'm frightened, Lord, and need your guidance as I try to make it on my own.*

For she knew in the bottom of her heart, she was truly alone. There would be no loving husband to comfort her as she tackled the challenges of motherhood nor would there be a proud father for the baby.

Faith closed her eyes and began to quietly sob.

Ella was silent as she rode with Noah to his new property.

Noah pulled into the driveway and turned to her. "I can't wait to show you the progress we've made on the house."

Ella could only smile faintly as he walked around to help her down from the buggy. How could she be excited when Faith was missing? How could she focus on her future with Noah when she didn't know if she would ever see her sister again? She didn't know how she was going to manage to be enthusiastic, but she knew she had to try, because Noah had spent many hours trying to set the property to rights.

Silence reigned between them as they walked up the sidewalk to the porch. Noah inserted the key in the lock and opened the heavy oak door. Ella stepped into the kitchen and gasped. New oak cabinets replaced the old pine cabinets that had been there before. Soft green paint covered the walls and new linoleum lay under her feet.

"So, what do you think? I wasn't sure what changes to make, but I hope you like it." Noah eyed her nervously.

"Noah," Ella said as a smile lit up her face, "I love it. I can't believe how much work you have accomplished in so little time. This must have taken you hours!"

Noah smiled. "I'm happy you like it. If there is anything you don't like, I'm willing to change it. I want you to be pleased with what is to be your future home."

"Thank you, Noah." Ella ran her hand over the smooth finish of the handcrafted cupboards. She knew it must have taken him hours to attain such perfection, the cupboards were absolutely beautiful.

She turned to smile at him. "I wouldn't change a thing, they are wonderful."

Noah breathed a sigh of relief. "Are you certain? I could make different ones if you don't like these."

Ella arched her brows and laughed. "My goodness, Noah. I hope you don't think I'm that picky. The cupboards are perfect and are made even more special, because you made them yourself. I will treasure them always."

Noah's cheeks flushed. "Thank you, Ella. The compliment means a lot coming from you."

Ella looked at the man who was her heart and soul. She couldn't imagine a future without him and she thanked the Lord for returning her to where she was meant to be all along.

She walked into the living room and squealed in delight at the newly refinished wooden floor and the sunlight streaming through the large windows. In her mind she began to picture where she would place furniture once she and Noah were married.

Noah walked into the room and surveyed it with a look of satisfaction. "I'm pleased with the way the floor turned out. I need to thank your father and grandfather again for spending so many hours helping me."

Ella walked over to the staircase and peered upstairs.

"You can go up and see the rooms," Noah said with a hint of a smile. "Luke has already picked out the room at the top of the stairs for his own, but there are three other bedrooms."

Now it was Ella's turn to blush.

Noah grinned mischievously. "If it makes you more comfortable, I will wait down here."

"Thank you, Noah," Ella murmured. With butterflies in her stomach, she climbed the stairs leading to the second floor. At the top of the stairs she paused and looked into the room that was to be Luke's. The walls had been freshly painted and the floorboards gleamed. Out the bedroom window the branches of a tall oak tree swayed and she could imagine it occupying the imagination of a little boy as he drifted off to sleep.

She walked further down the hall and peeked into sunny bedrooms on the right and the left until she reached the largest bedroom at the end of the hall. Nervously she walked into the room that was to be hers and Noah's in the future. Double windows graced the south wall and here, just like in the previous bedrooms, the floorboards shown.

Ella walked back downstairs and met Noah's questioning gaze.

"It's wonderful, Noah, just like the rest of the place. I can't believe how much you have gotten done in such a short time. You must have spent all of your free time setting this place to rights."

"*Jah*, it has been time consuming, that's for sure, but it is worth it. I can scarcely believe it is almost finished. Before too much longer, Luke and I will be moving into our very own home."

Ella walked over to give Noah a hug. "It will be an amazing place for both of you to live. You deserve to have some peace in your life."

"It will be an amazing place for *us* to live," Noah murmured as he brushed his lips against hers.

Ella couldn't agree with him more.

Chapter Twenty-seven

Noah faced his mother across the expanse of the kitchen. For the first time in a long time he truly looked at the woman who had given birth to him. When had she gotten so old? The years since his father and Caleb's deaths hadn't been kind and now she was experiencing another heartache.

"I don't want Ella Graber as a daughter-in-law, Son." Martha's expression soured as she finished putting away the clean dinner dishes. "Rebecca was the perfect wife for you. I thanked the good Lord the day you were married."

"That she was," Noah said quietly.

His mother stared down at the dish towel she clutched in her hand. "Don't get me wrong, I'm happy for Abram and Gretta that their oldest daughter has returned, but she doesn't belong in this family."

"But, *mamm,* Ella is the daughter of your best friend. Surely you can find it in your heart to forgive her." Noah hated pleading with his mother, but she was being unreasonable. The accident had been just that, an accident and even if it weren't, they were instructed by their faith to forgive.

Tears sparkled on Martha's lashes. "Don't you think I want to forgive? I have spent many a night in prayer asking God to soften my heart, but my prayers have been in vain."

Noah peeked into the family room. Luke was happily playing with his toys on the floor and seemed oblivious to the adult conversation that was taking place in the next room.

Martha sat down at the table and leaned forward wearily. "And what about Gideon? Now I have your younger *bruder* to worry about as well. Gretta may be my best friend, but she has done a poor job in parenting her daughters. Why, if Faith were my daughter, she wouldn't have been allowed to run wild. Now she is pregnant and has managed to steal Gideon away from his family."

Noah respected his mother far too much to roll his eyes. He knew that Gideon was just as much to blame for the entire mess, but decided to keep his opinion to himself. Instead, he decided to try a new approach.

"I've asked Bishop Burkholder to stop by this evening." His words fell like bricks between them.

His mother snapped to attention. "Why?"

Noah shifted on his feet, but held his mother's gaze. "I thought it might help for you to speak to him."

She furrowed her brow. "You haven't told him about Gideon and Faith?" she whispered, clearly worried.

He shook his head. *"Nee,* but he's bound to find out sooner or later. I asked him here, because I thought talking to him might help ease the grief you feel over Father and Caleb's deaths."

"You had no right, Son!" Anger flashed in his mother's eyes. "I am perfectly capable of working through my grief on my own, in my own time, without the help of the Bishop or anyone else for that matter."

Noah was relieved to hear the sound of buggy wheels on gravel. He walked to the door to greet the leader of their community.

Bishop Burkholder stepped into the kitchen. *"Gut* evening, Martha. Noah." He nodded at each of them in turn.

Noah excused himself leaving his mother alone with the bishop.

Martha offered the bishop a seat and winced when he sat in the chair that had been Silas's. She could still picture her late husband seated there, a twinkle in his eye as he talked about the day's events. Theirs had been a *gut* marriage filled with laughter and love. That was why she found it so difficult to forgive the woman responsible for extinguishing the lives of the ones she held so dear.

Bishop Burkholder gave her a serious look as she bustled around the kitchen, pouring him a cup of coffee and cutting him a generous wedge of apple pie. "Martha, please sit." He motioned to the chair she had vacated.

She sank heavily onto the chair in front of her, her fingers nervously toying with the coffee cup in front of her. "Noah told me why you are here."

His fork stilled halfway to his mouth. "Is that so?"

Martha nodded. "You came to lecture me about my treatment of the Graber girl."

"Ach, Martha, we've been friends a long time. Going on forty years now, ain't so?"

Martha allowed a faint smile to touch her lips. "Your family moved to LaGrange County the year I turned ten, if I remember correctly."

The Bishop nodded. *"Jah,* we've been friends since we were *kenner,* so why would you think I would lecture you now?"

Martha blinked rapidly as tears threatened. "I know my behavior has been wrong. It has been difficult for me to separate the woman she has become from the reckless teenager of long ago."

The Bishop leaned back in his chair and sighed. "You haven't forgiven her?"

"Nee," Martha said softly, "I haven't. Even though I've prayed plenty, I've yet to find peace."

"You know," the Bishop regarded her thoughtfully, "the Bible says if you forgive men when they sin against you, your heavenly Father will forgive you. But if you do not forgive, you yourself will not be forgiven."

Martha lowered her head in shame.

The Bishop gently continued, "Ella's *mamm* is a friend of yours, *jah?*"

"*Jah,*" Martha nodded. "Gretta is a *gut* friend."

"And it would make Gretta sad for you to continue feeling this way about her daughter, ain't so?"

"*Jah,*" Martha met his steady gaze, "I know Gretta is saddened by my unwillingness to forgive, but forgiving isn't always the easiest thing to do."

"*Nee,* it isn't," the Bishop agreed, "but I'm confident if you pray diligently, you will find an answer." He stood and prepared to leave. At the door, he turned and smiled warmly. "The girl I knew growing up was always quick to forgive. If you will search your heart, I'm sure you will find that girl."

Martha stood on the porch and watched as the bishop's buggy moved slowly down the drive. He had asked her to pray to God for help in healing her heart. To allow the healing balm of forgiveness to flow from her heart toward the woman who had taken ones she held so dear, but deep down she knew it was impossible. A bitterness had lodged in her soul that the mere passing of time could not erase.

"Please, Lord," she whispered, her soft words carried away on the wind. "Please let me forgive, forget and move forward with my life."

Chapter Twenty-Eight

The days turned into weeks and the day of Ella's baptism finally arrived. She awoke early, with dawn's light turning the shadows of the night to gray, then pink and finally the blue sky of a perfect spring day.

Excitement raced through Ella's veins as she leapt out of bed and quickly dressed. Today was the day she would promise to honor Christian values and follow the guidelines of the *Ordnung,* the rules of her church district.

The only cloud over the day was the absence of her younger sister, and Ella prayed that wherever Faith may be, she was safe and looking out for the well-being of her unborn child.

With a spring in her step, Ella walked downstairs and into the kitchen where her mother, grandmother and Holly had breakfast preparations well under way.

"Good morning, daughter." Her mother's face was wreathed in smiles. "It is a wonderful day for your baptism, ain't so?"

"*Jah,* the Lord has blessed us with a fine day." Ella walked over to give her mother a quick hug.

"It's going to be a long day." Corrine frowned as she walked into the kitchen carrying Grace. "Baptism Sundays always take forever."

"Now, Corrine," *Mamm* frowned. "You should be happy for your sister. Today is an important day in Ella's life."

"I am happy." Corrine offered Ella a half smile. "I just wish it wouldn't take so long, that's all."

Ella laughed and patted her younger sister's shoulder. "That makes two of us, but it is an important day and shouldn't be rushed."

Their father came in from his morning chores and walked over to give her a big hug. "This is an exciting day for you, *jah?*"

Ella nodded. "I didn't think I would be nervous, but I can't seem to calm the butterflies in my stomach."

"Ach, you will be fine," Holly waved away her concerns. "It will be over before you know it and then you will finally be a church member. I'm sure Noah thought this day would never come."

"Holly!" Ella blushed. "I'm sure, as a minister, Noah is happy I am joining the church."

"*Jah,*" Holly giggled. "I'm sure he will be."

"That is enough, Holly." *Mamm* swatted her daughter's arm. "Please don't tease your sister."

Their father sat down at the table and motioned for everyone to take their seats. After the silent blessing, breakfast past quickly and soon it was time to leave for church.

Ella watched the green fields roll by on the way to Samuel and Irene Hostetler's. Church was being held this Sunday in the Hostetler's spacious farmhouse and every available space would be occupied on this important occasion.

Today she would make a decision that would chart the course for the rest of her life. By joining the church she would be completing a step she had planned to make long ago, but the accident had changed all of that.

She briefly thought about Silas and Caleb and knew they would be happy for her on this special day.

The inside of the Hostetler's home was packed with members of their close-knit community and Ella received smiles and hugs from many of her long-time friends. She slowly made her way to the room where she would wait with the other young people who would also join the church this day.

After the hymns and sermons, Ella made her way to the front of the room and knelt. Tears filled her eyes as the bishop poured a cup of water over her head in the name of the Father, the Son, and the Holy Ghost.

She rose and received the holy kiss from the bishop's wife. Looking out over the congregation, her eyes fell upon Noah with Luke sitting safely by his side. A smile touched his lips and he nodded to her in approval.

Ella beamed back at him. She couldn't help, but think that today was the first day of the rest of her life.

Chapter Twenty-nine

Time flew quickly by and before long Indiana was mired in the sweltering days of August. Days were hot and humid and the nights were not much better.

Ella stepped out onto the porch in the dawn's breaking light and breathed in gulps of fresh air. Even at this early hour humidity hung thick in the air and the temperature hovered in the eighties.

Ella leaned against the porch railing and smiled as she thought about Noah. Just last week he and Luke had been able to move into their new home and he had never appeared happier.

A soft sound from the corner of the porch caused her to turn. She frowned at the whicker laundry basket that had been left sitting on the floor.

Surely they hadn't forgotten to bring in all of the clean clothes yesterday. Maybe Holly or Corrine had set the basket there and forgotten it.

Ella walked closer and frowned as she heard a faint whimper. Peering into the basket, she gasped. There, squinting up at her with big blue eyes lay a *boppli*. An envelope with Ella's name on it was pinned to the infant's blanket.

Ella reached for the envelope with trembling fingers. She opened it and pulled out a single sheet of paper.

Dear Ella,

As I sit here holding my precious daughter, Rose, I am struck anew at the kindness of our God. He has given me this dear, little life to love and watch over, but in my heart I know that I cannot.

Love, I can give, but Rose deserves to have a stable home and be surrounded by family.

As you may have guessed, Gideon and I are no longer together. He has no interest in being a father to our child and I cannot support her on what little I earn.

That is why I am turning to you. I have little choice, but to ask you to raise Rose as your own. I would ask mamm and daed, but know they have their hands full with Corrine and the grandbabies.

Please, Ella? Rose and I desperately need your help and there is no other choice.

Love, Faith

"You could have come home, Faith," Ella whispered as she stooped to pick up the basket. "You could have come home."

"What is that?" Corrine asked as Ella walked into the kitchen and deposited the basket onto the table.

"Did we forget to bring in all of the laundry?" Holly frowned.

"Nee." Ella shook her head and beckoned for everyone to come closer.

Their mother gasped as she peered into the basket. "What is a baby doing here? She turned to Ella with a question in her eyes.

Ella showed her mother the note. "This is Faith's daughter. Her name is Rose."

"Faith?" Her mother whirled toward the door. "Is she here?"

Ella placed a hand on her mother's arm. "No, mother, she isn't. Faith wasn't around when I found the basket sitting on the porch."

Her mother placed a hand over her heart. "Why on earth would Faith do such a thing? Why would she leave her baby sitting all alone on the porch?"

"Did someone mention Faith?" Their father walked into the kitchen wearing a puzzled frown.

"Faith left her *boppli* on the porch!" Corrine bounced up and down in excitement.

Their father walked over and looked into the basket at the infant who was gazing solemnly back at him.

He turned to his wife. "Is this true? Does this child belong to our Faith?"

"According to her note, Faith wants Ella to raise her daughter," Holly said as she scanned the sheet of paper. "And she and Gideon are no longer together."

Grandmother Graber shook her head. "That boy was always trouble."

"Why didn't she just come home?" *Mamm* wailed. "She could have raised her baby here. We would have welcomed her back. Surely Faith knows this will always be her home."

"Now, Gretta," their father murmured as he put his arms around his wife. "We need to thank the good Lord for giving Faith the common sense to bring the baby to a place where she knows it will be taken care of and loved. Faith will return home in her own time, but I am grateful she has entrusted us with the care of her daughter."

"She's sweet," Corrine said as she gazed at her niece. "She has blond hair just like Faith."

"Are you going to do as Faith has asked?" Holly gave Ella a curious look. "Are you going to raise her daughter?"

"Well, I…"

"Noah just pulled up outside," Corrine announced.

Their father glanced at the clock on the kitchen wall. "*Jah,* I guess it is time to begin work." He picked up a couple of biscuits off the platter sitting on the counter and split them open. Spearing a couple of slices of ham, he topped each sandwich off with a hard egg.

He stepped out onto the porch and said a few words to Noah.

Noah entered the kitchen.

"I guess my father told you about the baby?" Ella motioned to the basket on the table."

"*Jah,*" Noah nodded as he walked over to look at his niece. He smiled softly down at the infant who was now sleeping. "He also mentioned that Faith wants you to raise her?"

"Jah," Ella whispered, uncertain how the information would be received. "Faith asked me to raise her daughter as my own."

"What about Gideon?"

"They are no longer together and Faith said Gideon wants nothing to do with the baby."

Noah's jaw clenched, but he remained quiet for a moment. Then, as if he had come to a decision he turned to her.

"I guess this means we will need to ask the bishop if we can wed before the fall."

"Yipee! A wedding!" Corrine squealed.

"Hush, Corrine," *Mamm* did her best to frown, but wore a hint of a smile of her own. "Why don't we all go into the family room and give Noah and Ella some privacy."

Ella waited until her family had left the room then gazed up into Noah's solemn face. "What are you saying?"

Noah smiled softly. "The child is going to need a mother and a father, *jah?*"

Ella's hopes soared. "You are willing to be a father to Rose?"

"She named the baby, Rose?"

Ella nodded.

Noah's smile became broader. "Rose was my grandmother's name."

"Noah? You didn't answer my question. Are you willing to raise Rose as your own?"

He gently pulled her into his arms. *"Jah,"* he murmured before he placed a quick kiss on her lips. "I am."

Ella closed her eyes and said a quiet word of thanks. As she counted her blessings a scripture came to mind and she couldn't help, but smile for the Lord had been watching out for them all along.

The LORD is my shepherd; I shall not want.

Made in the USA
Middletown, DE
04 August 2015